INDIGO HILL

OTHER BOOKS BY LIZ ROSENBERG

Novels

The Laws of Gravity

The Moonlight Palace

Home Repair

Beauty and Attention

Biography

House of Dreams: The Life of L. M. Montgomery

Poetry

Children of Paradise

Demon Love

The Lily Poems

I Just Hope It's Lethal (anthology, coeditor Deena November)

INDIGO HILL

liz rosenberg

Author of *The Laws of Gravity*

This is a work of fiction. Names, characters, organizations, places, events, and incidents are either products of the author's imagination or are used fictitiously. Any resemblance to actual persons, living or dead, or actual events is purely coincidental.

Published by Lake Union Publishing, Seattle

www.apub.com

ISBN-13: 9781503904064
ISBN-10: 1503904067

Cover design by PEPE *nymi*

Printed in the United States of America

This book is dedicated to John Swenson and all his
family and Worcester friends who generously shared
their memory of events long past. In particular,
I need to thank the indomitable Ray Slater and
Phil Jakubosky for speaking with me at length and
answering my many questions. Special thanks to the
wonderful Mae Swenson, Dave Abare, Judi, Cate,
Bev, Dave, and Jeff, the godfather.
And sweet John, as you so often say, Thank you, thank you.

CHAPTER ONE

Alma Johansson was the most upbeat dying person at UMass Memorial, in the run-down Bell Hill area of Worcester. She wasn't happy to receive the grim diagnosis, of course, but she accepted the news calmly, with something like satisfaction, as her older daughter Louisa later remarked. After the doctor finished his long, careful explanations, when he'd offered his soft-spoken consolation and apologies—it was a shame they hadn't caught this sooner, though pancreatic cancer was a tough one—Alma nodded and smiled.

"I'm so glad I wasn't being a baby," she said. "I knew something was wrong."

Michelle and Louisa, her two grown daughters, were holding hands while this medical consultation took place, in a room barely large enough for all four chairs. They had not held hands since very early childhood, and seldom even then, as little girls. They were not so much holding hands now, as gripping each other's palms, trying to find something solid to hang on to. As soon as the doctor had finished speaking, Louisa let go. Tears sprang to Michelle's eyes—partly because of the terrible news, and partly from the pain of having her big sister pull away.

Alma insisted on going out for breakfast afterward with her two daughters, so they drove to the Parkway Diner, close to the hospital, though she'd had no appetite for weeks. A few regulars sat parked behind coffee cups at the counter, reeking of beer at ten in the morning.

Worcester grew alcoholics, Louisa's husband Art once said, the way abandoned fields grew weeds. Mrs. Johansson and her daughters took one of the diner's high-backed leather booths toward the back.

Louisa had been relieved to get in her car alone and drive away from the hospital. Well, you never really just drove, in downtown Worcester. You crawled along, one in a series of cars trying to navigate potholes and death traps.

The hospital sat on a hill. That was one building she was always glad to leave behind in her rearview mirror. She had always hated it. The hospital had changed considerably over the past almost thirty years—which had been the last time she'd spent any extended time at Memorial. But all the same, the place gave her a deep-down sick and queasy feeling. She couldn't ever forget approaching those glass doors as a teenager, week after week, each time with the same feeling of dread, heading over to the Burn Unit only to be told again to go away and come back in a few days. Come back in a week, young lady. Come back in a month. She had begged rides, and had even (though her parents didn't know about this part) hitchhiked from North Worcester just to stand in the same burn care lobby, arguing with the same soft-spoken nurses. Your friend isn't ready quite yet, dear. He needs his rest. Next time, call us first. And now here she was back at Memorial again, this time for her own mother.

It was a glum meal, in spite of Alma Johansson's relentless good cheer. Her elder daughter Louisa poked angrily at her Patriot Breakfast, featured on the cover of the glossy menu, while Michelle, the golden-haired baby of the family, refused anything more substantial than a cup of hot tea. She sipped it slowly, tears gliding down her face one by one, a few tears slipping into her cup.

"Remember the children's story about tear-water tea?" Alma asked, leaning forward on her elbows. "From that nice illustrated book, *Owl at Home*. I wonder where I put that book . . . You girls just loved that story. Do you remember?"

Michelle nodded, jabbing at her wet cheeks with a crumpled-up paper napkin.

"You loved all stories," Alma went on. "Oh, I wish I knew where I put that thing."

"Mom," Louisa interrupted, poking viciously at her eggs with her fork. "Why won't you at least *try* the chemo?"

"Oh, no," said Alma. "Not at my age. No indeed. I don't see the point."

"But you're only seventy-five! That's not old anymore."

"Your father died at seventy," Alma pointed out. Her eyes were bright blue and childlike.

"We all *know* that, Mom," Louisa said. She struggled to keep the irritation out of her voice, to restrain herself and stay calm. This was no time to get into an argument with her mother. Today, of all days, for Pete's sake. "But Dad died in a car crash. That was totally different."

"The doctor didn't seem to think chemo would do me much good." There was that same quality in her mother's voice again. Not exactly satisfaction, but something close, Louisa thought. As if she'd finally gotten a package in the mail for which she'd been waiting patiently a very long time.

Her mom laid her fork slantwise across the top of her mostly untouched plate. She had barely nibbled at her buttered rye toast. She had lost weight. Her appetite had been off for weeks, she'd been complaining of stomachaches, and Alma Johansson had never been a complainer. Louisa noticed with a pang that her mother's face looked sallow and slack, her high cheekbones yellowish instead of pink. How long had all this been going on? It was her job, as the eldest daughter, the responsible, sane one, to notice these things.

"Girls," their mother said briskly. "I'm sorry. I guess I just have a bad attitude. Your father, the great love of my life is gone, and I'm ready to join him. I wouldn't have chosen this, but then, we don't always get to choose."

"Oh, Mom," said Michelle, sliding her hand forward across the table to grasp her mother's hand.

Alma squeezed back, and the two of them sat there hand in hand across the table but Alma studied her elder daughter, Louisa, who stubbornly refused to meet her eyes, glaring instead at run-down Shrewsbury Street out the far window of the diner. Seemed like half the stores were empty these days. Soaped-up windows, sporting **FOR RENT** and **FOR SALE** signs.

Her mother's voice when she spoke was gentle. "I know you think I should try everything I can, Louisa. But I'm not a good candidate for surgery, and I hate the idea of chemo. Forgive me, girls. I want to die with my own hair." She touched her hair with her free hand, the waves still more blonde than white. She'd always had soft, pretty hair. She'd always been an attractive woman. "I just want to play out the hand I've been dealt."

"I think you have a wonderful attitude!" Michelle blurted out.

Louisa shot her sister a look. Another country heard from. "How's that again, now?"

"To be so accepting," said Michelle in a shaky voice. "I don't think it shows a bad attitude. I think Mom is—" And the tears came sliding down again. "—being very brave," Michelle whispered.

Louisa rolled her eyes.

"Well," her mother said. "I'm not afraid of death. That's the truth. I know I'll see your father again." She opened her eyes wider for an instant, as if to demonstrate. Her throat seemed to grow longer, and thinner. "I believe we'll find all our loved ones who have gone on long before us. My father and mother. My brother Oskar." She opened her eyes again, and looked almost merry. "So many people I'm looking forward to seeing!" Michelle couldn't help laughing along with her mother. Their high voices rang out. One or two nearby diners glanced over and smiled at the pair. Just another happy family reunion.

Two chuckle-headed idiots, Louisa thought. She'd been all alone in this family, the lone kangaroo, ever since her sensible father had been killed in that car crash, seven years earlier. Maybe even longer. Louisa had always been the odd one out. Her father wouldn't have argued with either of them about trying the chemo. He wouldn't have insisted on doing the sane, responsible thing. He'd just have said, whatever your mother wants, tossing up his hands.

"I know you're disappointed," Alma murmured apologetically.

"Eh, well." Louisa laid down her fork with a clatter. She glared at it as if the silverware itself were to blame. Sometimes an evil genie took over Louisa's middle-aged body. She found herself acting like a teenager again. Having fits, sulking. Louisa threw her napkin onto her plate, done with the meal. She was too fat, anyway. Soft and out of shape. She and her husband Art, both. "It won't be the first time I've been disappointed. And I don't suppose it will be the last, either."

She felt, rather than saw, the look of agonized appeal that her younger sister shot her way. It was Michelle's *Please Be Nice* look. Louisa ignored it, but ignoring it brought her smack up against her mother's clear china-blue gaze, taking her in.

"No," her mother said gently. "I'm sure it won't be, the last."

~

The end came sooner for Mrs. Johansson than anyone could have predicted. The outlook had been bleak from the start. Pancreatic cancer was a hard one to beat, and Alma's disease was advanced by the time they found it. Dr. Welch talked to them about a matter of months, time enough to get all of Mrs. Johansson's affairs in order, but in fact she lasted less than two weeks. Thirteen days from diagnosis to her death. Those few days passed by in a blur. It was a mercy, friends said; Alma had gone without pain or fear. Michelle was relieved her mother hadn't suffered, but even so . . . it was a shock. Her mother was not the kind of person to rush into or out of anything.

The sisters hadn't had time for a proper goodbye. There were no formal gatherings. No farewell ceremonies. Theirs was a small family to begin with. Over time it had shrunk down still further. Louisa was childless, and Michelle had just the one daughter, Sierra, who was herself unwell, with type 1 juvenile diabetes. There wasn't much extended family left, not in Worcester, not anywhere. The mother and her daughters hadn't said the kinds of useful, profound things people say at such times—or what Michelle imagined people said, because she had no firsthand experience of long goodbyes. In retrospect, it became even more important, the fact that they'd never had those final heart-to-heart mother-and-daughter talks.

They did come close to such a conversation, one morning shortly after the cancer diagnosis. The three women had gathered at Alma's Formica kitchen table on Ararat Street in North Worcester, the house Alma had lived in for more than forty years. It was where the two sisters had grown up, played together under the kitchen table, argued as teenagers, and drifted away. Did everything momentous have to happen around a kitchen table? It seemed so to Michelle. At this same kitchen table, they had all heard about the friends who had died in that terrible accident up at Indigo Hill. Someone had tossed gasoline onto an open flame and the whole place had gone up like tinder. They had tried without success to console Louisa here, sitting rigid in her chair as if she'd been turned to stone. At this same spot at the table, looking out over these same place mats, Michelle had proudly announced her engagement to Joe Hiatt, more than a decade ago, showing off her diamond engagement ring. Her mom had sat in the same kitchen chair, at the same place, facing the window that opened onto Indigo Hill, year after year, doing the *Telegram* crossword puzzle, reading her mail, checking their homework, clipping coupons, passing the applesauce. She looked the same now as she always had, just slightly thinner, with her apron removed. She was neatly dressed in slacks and a polyester blouse printed over with tiny blue flowers.

Mrs. Johansson always loved it when one or the other of her girls, as she still called them, stopped by for morning coffee. Alma Johansson, capable and adept in a hundred ways, had never yet managed to decode the intricate mysteries of a coffee maker. If one of "the girls" failed to come by and brew real coffee for her, she'd make the crystallized instant stuff out of a jar, with a spoonful of powdered dairy creamer. In truth, she never seemed to taste the difference. Still, the sisters took turns brewing her real coffee, several days a week. It was one of the few things Alma would allow them to do for her. All her life, Alma had been doing things for others. This time both sisters came together.

"Now isn't this nice," Alma said, looking affectionately at her daughters. "All three of us here together again." She sighed happily, smoothing her hand over the lace tablecloth.

"What are you going to do today, Mom?" asked Michelle. She worried that with so little to keep her occupied, her mother might start fretting and brooding about what lay ahead.

"Oh, well." Her mother waved both hands slowly and vaguely over the table, as if casting a spell. "You know . . . the usual."

She would do what she'd been doing for the last seven years, ever since her husband had passed away. She'd putter around the house, finish as much as she could of the Worcester *Telegram* crossword puzzle; polish off whatever coffee was left in the pot, carry a few cookies upstairs, and watch old war movies and romances till two in the morning. What did Michelle expect her mother to do, Louisa wondered irritably. Take up astrophysics? Start tap-dancing?

"I wish I had a little more time," her mother said matter-of-factly. "I wanted to be there at Sierra's wedding."

If she ever has a wedding, Michelle thought, an idea she brushed aside like a spider's web. Of course her daughter would get married. She was a lovely, lovable girl. Sierra's numbers were good these days. They were making strides with type 1 diabetes, improving the monitors and insulin pumps. And maybe even her mother would surprise them all . . .

"And you," her mother had said, turning to Louisa. "I still think you ought to have children."

"Oh for heaven's sake," said Louisa crabbily. "I'm forty-three years old. I'm almost menopausal."

"There's always adoption," her mother said, dropping her hands into her lap. "Lots of nice families adopt. Some of the very nicest. You'd see, Louisa, it would change your life. You were always such a happy baby, yourself."

Michelle laughed, out of sheer surprise, and Louisa snorted. *Michelle* was the happy child. She was the easygoing, golden-haired smiley one. Louisa had been born cranky. Everybody knew that.

"Yes indeed," their mother insisted. "I never saw a calmer or happier baby in all my life. And your toothless little smile was just radiant. Strangers used to remark on your good temper. They'd stop the carriage to make comments. You never fussed, not till you were a year old. Why do you think we had Michelle so soon after?"

"I don't know, Mom," said Louisa. "I figured she was an antidote."

"Nonsense!" said Alma briskly. She brushed a few invisible crumbs from her tablecloth with her fingertips. "You were easy compared to most. A wonderful, happy baby. I'd like to see you acting that way again. Why, you used to giggle aloud in your sleep!"

"Sure, Mom," said Louisa, frowning.

"You did!"

"Whatever you say, Mom."

Alma Johansson sighed. She moved the salt and pepper shakers around, then swapped them back. Her sigh carried affection, resignation, regret, maybe just plain weariness. The blue veins bulged on the back of her hands and she looked down at them with apparent interest.

"There are so many things I'd love to tell you girls, but, well—I just don't know . . ." their mother said slowly. "It's so hard to know where to begin . . ." She tapped her fingers on a place mat in front of her. Her fingers danced softly, as if to a song buried inside her head.

"What kinds of things?" Michelle asked, intrigued, when out of nowhere her sister brusquely interrupted.

"Never mind all that," said Louisa.

Her mother looked surprised and hurt. Then something else came down behind her large blue eyes, like the shutter on a camera. Something habitual, Michelle realized later. An instinctive gesture of retreat. In the blink of an eye, the instant happened, then it was over. Her mom smiled at her two grown daughters.

"Go on upstairs and get some rest," ordered Louisa. "We'll talk another time. You look all tuckered out."

"Do I?" asked their mother mildly. She reached for another cookie. Mrs. Johansson had a terrible sweet tooth, even now that her appetite for real food was almost entirely gone. Every day in her house had always been *Lördagsgodis*—traditionally candy Saturday, for the Swedes. She'd kept bags of sweets secreted around the house. She even drove around with plastic bags of Tootsie Pops in the back of the car; rolls of Smarties in the glove compartment. Now she set two double-stuffed Oreos on a cracked flowered plate with a gold rim. The cracks didn't matter, she had once explained to her daughters, if you were only eating cookies.

After their mother had gone upstairs, the familiar sound of her footsteps creaking overhead, the two sisters sat another minute or two, looking at each other in silence. Words never got you anywhere with Louisa, Michelle knew. There was no point complaining, or saying that Louisa had just spoiled a precious moment.

"What?" demanded Louisa.

"Nothing," said Michelle, and she began to wash the dishes. You couldn't fight with Louisa because you couldn't ever win. Whatever their mother had wanted to confide in them would simply have to wait for another day.

Except there was no other day. The day for confidences never arrived. The very next morning Mrs. Johansson woke disoriented and achy, saying things that made no sense, and hospice increased her pain medication. She was groggy and out of it all afternoon, talking about foreign people and places they'd never before heard her mention. That night Alma fell asleep before dark, and she never again woke up fully.

The rate at which Alma Johansson's condition deteriorated shocked even the doctors, and the hospice staff that came and went into the house on Ararat with no apparent schedule. Time slipped loose. The clock suddenly ran on twenty-four hours, with no clear distinction between day and night. There was no final goodbye for any of them, just a fast, steady slipping away. The hospice people moved the patient downstairs, into one of those steel-barred hospital beds.

Mrs. Johansson slept on and on, out of reach behind the bars. She began to look like a shell when the animal has left it behind. Her fair hair shone against the white pillow. She barely stirred, and the nurses had to move her periodically to make sure she didn't get bedsores. Alma appeared to be sinking deeper under the weight of the thin cotton blankets. Michelle half expected to come by one morning and find her mother's body lodged into the bottom of the mattress.

Alma Johansson returned to consciousness only once and briefly, on the very last day of her life. Michelle was the one sitting downstairs by her side, alone, as close to her mother as she could get with the metal bars of the hospital bed in the way between them. She sat quietly knitting a scarf for her teenaged daughter Sierra. From time to time she glanced at her mother, who continued her long uneasy rest. It was late in the year, midway into April—scarf and hat season was almost over in Worcester, though you never knew for sure, you might have snow flurries in May. Or you could have an unseasonable New England heat wave that would carry you straight on into summer, with no spring at all. But Michelle had found a nice, soft hand-dyed knitting yarn, in a pretty mix of purples and blues, and the sixteen-year-old Sierra exclaimed over it in a way she hardly ever got excited about anything these days—anything that wasn't found on her phone or her computer.

Mrs. Johansson didn't seem to be asleep exactly. Neither was she quite awake. Michelle thought of someone floating on her back in a swimming pool. She could almost picture blue water.

"Mom?" Michelle ventured. "Mom, are you there?" It seemed suddenly lonely there in the house.

Michelle laid down her knitting needles. She felt foolish, but she pushed on anyway. No one had prepared them for any of this. Not the doctor, not even the nice hospice staff. If she was talking to herself, so be it. "I love you, Mom," Michelle said—something she'd hardly ever said aloud when her mother was alert and awake. The Johanssons, like most Worcester Swedes, were not a touchy-feely family. They didn't talk about their affections. They didn't make speeches.

"I love you very much," Michelle said, "and I always will. I just want you to know that."

Alma Johansson turned her head then and opened her eyes wide. She looked surprised. Before Michelle could read her mother's expression, her eyes closed again, the eyelids coming down over the bright-blue gaze. Her mother was breathing raggedly, almost panting; she appeared to be in some kind of physical distress. The hospice people would probably not be arriving for another hour. Michelle didn't know what she was supposed to do next. She didn't know how to ease her mother's discomfort. No one had given her any instructions. She was the helpless one, the baby of the family. Michelle scooched her chair forward six inches, lowered the metal bars on the hospital bed, leaned in, and wrapped her arms tightly around her mother. She laid her head down into the smell of the clean white linens as if hiding there, and folded her arms tightly around her mother like wings. Her mother's breathing made a loose rattling sound. Michelle was afraid to look up—afraid to watch her mother struggling with real trouble or pain. So she simply hung on; as long as her mother had difficulty breathing, as long as her muscles were tense, Michelle held on as tight as she could. Finally, after what seemed like a very long time, she felt her mother relax, the harsh breathing stopped, and at last Michelle let go.

Alma Johansson slept the deep sleep of the dreamless. Michelle waited a few more minutes, but nothing else changed or moved. Every object in the room seemed fixed in its place—the cluster of old family photographs, furred around the edges with dust; a high pile of out-of-date newspapers; the many small china figurines; her mother's collection of toothpick holders, some of them made of china, others of wood or plastic. Michelle wasn't absolutely sure her mother was still breathing. The sunlight shone through her mother's thin white curtains. After what seemed like a very long while, she heard the key turn in the front door lock, and the nice woman from hospice hung up her wool spring coat in the crowded hall closet, with a familiar scraping sound of metal on metal, the hanger squeaking across the pole. Only then was it clear that Alma was already gone.

CHAPTER TWO

When the lawyer's office over in West Boylston called the family to arrange for the reading of the will a few days after the burial, they suggested that each of the daughters bring someone along to be there with them, a close friend or loved one.

"What for?" asked Louisa, but the secretary didn't offer a satisfactory explanation. Michelle invited her husband, Joe, to accompany her, but Louisa said of her own husband, "Art's not any good at this kind of thing. Besides, they're just covering their own behinds. Maybe they're scared we'll make a scene in their office. Boo-hoo. Some people are just so ridiculously emotional."

This dig was aimed at her, Michelle knew. And it was true—she had been carrying on tearfully, weeping and leaking like a sieve ever since the day her mother died. Michelle hadn't cried this much since she was a little girl. Maybe not even then. She'd been feeling as off balance as if someone had shoved her from behind. She was not recognizably herself anymore, not without her mom.

She worried about what her daughter must think—Sierra, a type 1 diabetic, had enough on her plate. The way Michelle carried on, she feared she wasn't setting a good example. She should act more grown-up. But somehow she couldn't manage to pull herself together. It felt as if the very center of her being had fallen away. Michelle hadn't grieved this way even when her father was killed—partly because of the shock of the accident, and because they'd all been so busy holding her mother together. No one could then afford the luxury of grief. Now she went to sleep sniffling damply into Joe's warm shoulder and woke with tears already sliding from her eyelids. And the one person in the world that she needed most, the only one who could have comforted and understood her loss, was her own mother, nowhere to be found.

But Sierra, who at age sixteen had plunged into her hard-hearted cranky years, acted unusually gentle and sympathetic at this time. If she thought her mother was acting *weird* a favorite word she kept it to herself. She didn't grouse about her math and social studies homework. She didn't complain. She did her chores and monitored her own insulin pump without being hounded. Michelle saved the message on her cell phone voice mail where Sierra had called in tears to say she'd heard that Grandma had died. Michelle hardly ever heard that voice anymore—the openly emotional, loving one, the voice of a child. But Sierra had to be protected, too. She'd recently gone into a worrisome dark goth phase—wearing torn black leggings, heavy black eye makeup, listening to heavy-metal music late into the night, her pretty golden-brown hair chopped short, dyed black, and slicked back stiff as a helmet.

"I won't blubber," Michelle assured Louisa. "And I won't make a scene, either. I promise." But the lawyer's request, to bring someone else along to the law office, struck her as odd and worrisome. It was the kind of thing they told you to do at a hospital when the person you were coming to see had already died.

"Isn't that unusual?" she asked her husband Joe, who was a lawyer himself. But Joe handled environmental issues almost exclusively. He didn't deal with family law.

"I'm not sure," said Joe. "All I know is, I'm happy to come to the office with you." Joe was lucky. Both his father and his stepmother were alive and well. They still led busy lives. His father drove his own car, a blue-green Cadillac, though he was into his eighties. Joe belonged to a big, noisy, tight-knit Jewish family right there on the West Side, all of them within a few blocks of each other. They walked to the synagogue together. His father played twenty-seven, sometimes thirty-six holes at Tatnuck Country Club, most days in season. Any day when it wasn't snowing or the greens weren't frozen solid. Joe's mother played mah-jongg and belonged to a book group at the JCC on Salisbury Street. Michelle realized with a jolt that she herself was now an orphan.

The April weather had turned nasty. Michelle woke to the sound of New England sleet striking the window, as if someone were throwing pebbles against the glass. It made her feel even more sick at heart to think of her mother alone out there under the bleak elements. Michelle wiped the tears away, put on some makeup to cover the evidence of her crying, and dressed in her winter clothes. Something sober, but not too funereal. She didn't want to get Louisa started.

Michelle had called in for a half-day's personal leave to attend the lawyer's meeting; she was a part-time reading specialist in the Worcester Central elementary schools. She'd gone from full-time to part-time when Sierra was born, and somehow never made it all the way back into the classroom. She wasn't even sure she'd like to teach full-time anymore. School just wasn't much *fun* these days. It seemed to her that all the exhausted teachers did anymore was to fill out more forms and jump through administrative hoops and hand out standardized tests, even to the very littlest children. Even to kindergarteners, who were just getting adjusted to being away from home and learning to tie their shoes and use the bathroom by themselves. It used to be that the youngest elementary school children blithely colored pictures and played games and sang songs. Now it was grind, grind, grind, and Lord help the child who wasn't reading whole books alone by first grade. And God help the teacher who hadn't performed miracles to get them reading. Never mind if the child came to school hungry or sick or in torn, filthy clothes—or didn't come to school at all. Somehow these days everything was always made out to be the teacher's fault.

"Do I look all right?" Joe asked her, standing in the bedroom doorway. He wasn't sporting his usual "go-to-meeting clothes," as he called his everyday lawyer suits. Joe always went to work in elegant suits, with Brooks Brothers no-iron blue shirts, and solid or striped silk ties.

Today he was wearing baggy blue sweatpants and a long-sleeved polo shirt, a pair of sneakers and a baseball cap. At least the cap wasn't on backward, Michelle thought. He looked much as he had when Michelle met him at college, a few more lines on his face, a touch of gray at the temples. He seemed so happy in that goofy outfit she couldn't bring herself to tell him that no, of course he should not wear sweatpants. No man should ever wear sweatpants, she believed—any more than they should wear skimpy shorts, or a fanny pack. But there was that shy Joe smile, in a V shape.

"You look beautiful," she declared, kissing him on the mouth.

"Bundle up. I'll warm up the car," he told her. After twenty years, Joe still lay on Michelle's side of the bed to warm her sheets while she brushed her teeth. Her father had once called Joe Hiatt "the goodest man" he'd ever known. Joe volunteered at his West Side synagogue, coached a girls' basketball team, gave large sums to charity, and performed a hundred other secret good deeds. He was the one who cheerfully showed up at 5:00 a.m. when an extra parent was needed, the sticky man running the cotton candy booth at the school dances. (After Sierra was diagnosed with diabetes, he had campaigned for healthy snacks, and now manned the deserted fresh fruits and vegetables station instead.) He was more than a lover, more than a friend, but the best of these as well. Michelle was lucky to have him, luckier than anyone could ever know—and then she felt guilty for calling herself lucky when her one and only mother lay dead under the blowing snow.

"Oh, give yourself a break," she said aloud.

~

It was not old Mr. Enright, their parents' lawyer of many years, who stepped out into the spacious West Boylston law office lobby to greet them, but his young son, Eddie. The office, right off of Prospect Street, now had one of those elegant, carved gold-rimmed hand-painted signs you saw all over Cape Cod. The lobby, once a musty, cramped dark and narrow space, was now open and sunlit, with clerestory windows and a crystal chandelier sparkling overhead.

It turned out that Mr. Enright Senior had retired two years earlier. Now it was his son's practice, apparently. Little Eddie Enright! Louisa shook her head over him, disapprovingly, as if he'd shown up in short pants, while the young lawyer murmured his condolences, shaking each of their hands in turn, pausing a moment to hold their hands in both of his own. "I'm so sorry for your loss," he told each sister, in a baritone voice that surprised them. The last time they'd known him he was a tiny kid, with a high, fluting voice and a weakness for jelly beans.

Michelle had babysat now and again for Eddie Enright back in high school. She remembered him clearly as a chubby little boy. Back then he'd been addicted to a cartoon program called *Little Einsteins*, and to reruns of the *Power Rangers*. She could picture him sitting cross-legged on the floor of his den, nibbling handfuls of Pepperidge Farm Goldfish and watching TV. Now she supposed he was in his early thirties. It made her feel ancient, at forty-one. He wore a plain thick gold band on his left hand—so young Eddie Enright was married—maybe with cartoon-watching children of his own.

He must not have been in practice long, however, because he looked hopelessly awkward and ill at ease with his new clients. His prematurely bald head was sweating so that it shone under the chandelier. His face had a sickly greenish-white cast.

"Relax!" Michelle was tempted to tell him. "Cheer up!" As Sierra would have said, *Take a chill pill.* Later Michelle was grateful she hadn't said anything at all.

He led them down a long hallway. They silently pulled out their chairs in the stuffy conference room, under bright lights, and sat down around a smallish table. It looked like they were all assembled there to play cards, maybe a game of Pitch.

Their young lawyer sighed. "This is very difficult," Eddie Enright began after a longish silence, staring down at his large folded hands.

"Well, the worst is over," said Louisa brusquely. "Our mother didn't suffer. I have clients coming at noon." You had to know Louisa to know she wasn't completely heartless. Far from it. She'd always been, if anything, too soft hearted for her own good. She was a mental-health counselor over at We Are U.S. of A. Her clients adored her.

"All right, then," Eddie said, flustered. "Let's get down to it. Most wills are relatively straightforward. Others are a bit more . . . complex." He flipped open a manila folder and sighed at it. The greenish-white color in his face was back. Michelle was afraid he might be sick. He took a handkerchief from his pocket and mopped his face and neck. "Whew. Let's see, now."

"We're grown-ups. We're not going to fall apart," said Louisa. "*Are* we, Michelle?"

"No," Michelle said meekly.

"So let's get this show on the road," said Louisa, drumming her fingers on the table.

"Your mother's will falls somewhere in the middle," said Eddie Enright methodically. Had he always talked this slowly? "She has left you two ladies all of the monies and properties, her IRA account, and most of her annuities . . ."

"Most?" interrupted Louisa.

Eddie continued to stare down at the paperwork, picking up speed as he went along. "She's also left you the house on Ararat Street, of course, with the proceeds of the sale, should you so choose, to be evenly divided between sisters. She seems to have left a few pieces of jewelry to Sierra—your daughter, I think?" he added, turning to Michelle.

Michelle nodded, her eyes filling with tears despite the dirty look Louisa was shooting her across the table. "Other than that, everything goes to you and your sister equally—with two small exceptions . . . There is one annuity otherwise designated. And the material contents of her home." Eddie stopped, mopped the back of his neck, and shot Michelle an agonized look she recalled from when she would declare it was his bedtime.

He didn't attempt to meet Louisa's glare at all.

"The annuity and contents of the house have been left to a Michael T. Birch who when last known lived in Cornwall, England. He is your mother's eldest child. In fact—her son."

This news was received in stunned silence for a few seconds.

Then Louisa burst out. "That's crazy! Our mother didn't have a son."

"I'm so very sorry," said little Eddie Enright. "I know this must come as quite a shock."

It was exactly what Dr. Welch had said when he first broke the bad medical news to their mother. Stage IV pancreatic cancer. Louisa remembered it clearly, as if the memory had been engraved in her brain. Same exact words. The same mild, practiced tone of voice. I know this must come as quite a shock.

"What are you *talking* about?" Louisa demanded. "There is no son. Our mother had two children. Both daughters." She wagged a finger back and forth between herself and her sister Michelle. "Us. That's it! We're it."

"So terribly sorry," said Eddie, shaking his head.

"There must be some mistake." Joe Hiatt spoke in his deep lawyerly everybody-let's-calm-down voice. But his thick black eyebrows had shot so far up they'd disappeared beneath the brim of his baseball cap. Michelle might have laughed if it hadn't all been so terrible.

"There's a good deal of legal documentation," said Eddie. "A very thorough paper trail. Your mother was diligent. Birth certificate, notarized papers, the adoption papers for the family in Cornwall; they're all here . . . Of course my father drew up the original will long ago. I even have a few photographs. Would you like to see a picture of your brother?" he asked no one in particular.

"No!" shouted Louisa. "We don't *have* a brother. Okay? This is our mother you're talking about. Our *dead mother*!"

"Calm down," said Michelle in a faint voice. She could barely be heard. It felt as if the whole room were tilting. Things were out of whack. *She*, Michelle, was the emotional one, the baby. *She* was the one always being told to simmer down.

"Why should I calm down! Don't tell me to calm down!" yelled Louisa, waving her arms. "This is terrible! It's incredible—and it's horrible."

"Well, it's a big surprise," said Michelle soothingly, "but it's not the end of the world."

Joe edged his chair a little closer to Eddie's at the head of the table. He'd put on his reading glasses and was already going through the legal paperwork. He lifted up and studied a photograph.

"Oh, yes it is!" said Louisa. Her voice sounded strangled. Louisa had the strangest expression on her face, like she was trying to work out a difficult math problem. Her eyebrows worked up and down. "It *is too* the end of the world!" Then she burst into tears.

CHAPTER THREE

Louisa parked her Chevy outside her own house, a neat, bland little gray ranch house at the edge of the nicer neighborhoods of the West Side of Worcester. On her street the homes were all crowded together, with tiny side yards and even smaller square backyards. The houses to her looked as if they were clinging by their fingernails to the vestiges of elegance from the nicer broader avenues on the West Side.

She switched off the ignition at the curb. Her car ticked like a clock when she shut off the engine. But she didn't go inside. She just couldn't. She couldn't face the blank emptiness of her own house. All those dull neutral colors Art insisted on, the muffling wall-to-wall beige carpeting. No windows open, not a single current of moving air. It would feel like entering a tunnel alone. The very idea of it made her feel short of breath. Michelle had tried to warn her off buying this house. "It's so not you!" she cried. "Why would you live here?" Joe was rich, Michelle had no idea about money. Louisa and Art had scrimped and saved to be able to buy this. They were still working like dogs to pay it off. Sometimes Louisa wondered why they bothered. Art was off working at his office at Sloane's Manufacturing in North Worcester. It was only five miles away, but it might as well have been five hundred miles.

Everyone in the Johansson family, as far back as Louisa could remember, had worked at the Sloane's Manufacturing company at some point or another, including her own mother and father and both of her grandfathers and great-grandfathers. She'd done a summer job of secretarial work at Sloane's herself, the year she turned sixteen. Some of the jobs over there at Sloane's were terrible; others were worse. One grandfather had worked in the rubber wheel and his clothes had always smelled of burning rubber; another had sweated out his labor in the infamous hot press. "The Heart of the Commonwealth," as the city fathers and PR people liked to call it, Worcester was a city of machinists. Some would say it had been in a state of slow decline for the past fifty years. And 2008 had not been a good year for anyone. They'd been trying to fix up the downtown convention center for decades. Of course, Sloane's hadn't been the same place either, since the manufacturing company changed hands. A Dutch corporation had taken over a few years earlier—supposedly the white knight of corporate rescue, but it hadn't quite turned out that way.

Instead, they had issued in a series of heavy layoffs, some employees being fired for good reasons but most for no reason at all—and Art in Human Resources was the stooge who had to call in some diligent worker who'd labored at Sloane's for twenty-five, thirty years, and ladle out the bad news and the severance package. Not a terribly generous package, either.

Now that the housing market had taken such a heavy hit it seemed like the city of Worcester, their county, all of the Northeast, in fact the entire country was falling apart. No wonder Art was so down at the mouth these days. All he did was eat and worry. Nothing pleased him anymore, nothing made him happy. This latest news sure wouldn't help.

Louisa sat with her car keys balanced in her gloved palm, reviewing her outburst in the law office. She hadn't carried on like that in twenty years—in such a passionate storm of tears. She hadn't broken down sobbing when her beloved dog Mo died; hadn't raged over the sudden deaths of her father or her mother. Life was full of nasty jolts and surprises. Louisa figured she should be used to that by now. She'd known it a long time. People disappointed you. They let you down, they went away or died. They seldom turned out the way you thought.

But not, whispered the secret voice in her head, not your *mother*. Not Alma Johansson, the favorite mom among all her friends. Never the steady, even-tempered woman who had been the smiling center of strength and calm, the bastion of *sameness* all her whole life. Her mother at least could be counted on; Alma Johansson was rock solid—or so Louisa had always believed. Louisa wasn't religious, it wasn't a matter of faith. She didn't go to church. Her people were not especially devout; they attended church at Christmas and Easter and that was enough. You almost didn't need a religion when you had a mother like Alma around.

Louisa studied the circle of keys resting in her hand as if they held the secret to some deep mystery. They sat shining and sharp edged and tangled in the center of her winter glove. She could drive the five miles to Sloane's offices of course; Art would take a few minutes out of his harried day to talk to her. He might look exasperated, he might sigh and look at his watch, but he'd do it. They'd sit in one of those little gray rooms, on gray folding metal chairs, around a long metal table, with a half-open box of bad chain-store donuts . . . She could picture the fluorescent lights flickering and buzzing overhead.

Art would be disappointed by this unexpected turn of events, possibly even shocked by the news. He had practically worshipped his mother-in-law Alma. He'd purse his lips, shake his head in dismay. No. No way. She just couldn't do it. Louisa stuck the key into the ignition, and before she knew it she had parked her Chevy in the lot behind the hardware store belonging to her oldest school friend, Flick Bergstrom.

The sight of the old familiar brick building made her breathing a little easier, the pain at the center of her chest less intense.

Bells jingled overhead as she pushed through the door. Old-fashioned Christmas-type sleigh bells. A comforting, happy sound. She saw Flick standing toward the back of the store, tall and lanky behind the counter. As soon as Flick spotted Louisa's stricken face, he scowled, plunked down the carton of saw blades he'd been pricing with a price gun, and barked, "Come outside."

Louisa and Flick had known each other close to forty years. They'd met back in kindergarten, at Indigo Hill School where both were drawn to the Quiet Corner, which strangely enough, had housed an old record player. Even then, Flick was crazy about music. He grabbed a cap now, with **BERGSTROM'S** written in white against dark-blue cotton and jammed it down on his narrow head. It was midmorning in midspring but Flick still suffered bad scarring from the fire he'd been in as a teenager, and he couldn't take any sun at all. Not even the weak watery New England sun in early April. That was why he'd moved back north from Georgia after his second divorce. "Come outside with me," he said.

Despite the terrible scarring—it ran like a broken river all over the right side of his face, down his neck, across his shoulder and who knew where else—Felix Bergstrom was still the handsomest man Louisa had ever known, in real life, outside of the movies or TV. He'd also been the handsomest teenager, and the cutest boy in her elementary school. When he stretched his long legs out in front of him, like he was doing now, settling himself into a shady corner on the back stoop of his store, your stomach could do swoops and dives just looking at his body settling into place, the smooth muscles pulling in his arms . . . if you were the kind of woman who experienced that type of swooping and diving, which emphatically Louisa was not.

Louisa knew plenty of girls like that. She'd gone to school with a few too many of them; they were all over Worcester, middle aged but still giggling, hanging out in bars; flirting and putting on too much mascara, with their potbellies and stretch marks and all the rest of it. Put them around an unattached man like Flick and they acted like deer at a salt lick.

Flick had never had to lift a finger to summon them, yet the females all came running. First Flick's own mother, a single divorced mom, had doted on him, then his women teachers, and after that, one by one his female classmates fell into place. He'd never really known his father, who'd died young, keeling over suddenly behind the counter of Bergstrom's hardware store. Heart attack. Flick's given name was Felix, but a younger brother couldn't pronounce it, so the nickname stuck. It suited him—suggested something quick as a lit match, something you couldn't quite pin down. He and Louisa had been friends forever, they were in all likelihood still best friends now, but Louisa couldn't say she ever knew for sure what Flick was thinking, or what decision he'd make next. The only thing you could be sure of was that he'd shrug and smile and make a bad one, given the choice.

Louisa and Flick were part of the loyal Gang of Six that still met for breakfast every Saturday morning at the Kenmore Diner or at Lou Roc's on Boylston Street—part of the sometimes considerably larger group graduated from Burncoat High that went out for dinner and Trivia Wednesday nights at Moynihan's. Art showed up just for the breakfast some weekends, grudgingly, because he didn't care for Trivia, and Art was exhausted in the evenings these days. He didn't bother to hide it, either. His feet dragged. His shoulders stooped like a much older man. Art had never been terribly high energy to begin with.

Louisa had known Art Wandowski almost as long as she'd known Flick. He'd been a chubby tagalong in the outer circle of their group of friends. Art grew up in a falling-down apartment house, what they called a three-decker on Andover Street. He was one of those kids you just naturally overlooked. Flick lived a few blocks farther away, on Brattle Street, in the old neighborhood. They'd all known each other for what felt like a lifetime. Greater Worcester was the City of Ten Colleges, and every one of Louisa's group of friends had either skipped college or gone to one of the local ten. Louisa herself had attended Worcester State, and was an indifferent student. Her sister Michelle had gone to Holy Cross on a tennis scholarship. Flick had graduated from Assumption College, just barely scraping by. Those were Flick's worst drinking days. Of course that was right after the fire, and it was a miracle he was still alive at all. He hadn't even been expected to survive. Art on the other hand had skipped college entirely and gone straight to work.

"What's up?" said Flick, shifting around on the stoop to get comfortable. He was always in pain, because of the damage he'd sustained from the fire. He had suffered burns over something like 30 percent of his body. If he felt lousy, he hid it well. Flick was all arms and legs, with a long crooked nose and stormy blue eyes that changed color all the time and a sharp chin and you wouldn't have thought the combination of those features would be appealing, but somehow it was. His voice had that raspy edge to it that some male singers had, a raggedness that always made them seem like they were at the edge of expressing some deep, desperate emotion. If so, with Flick it sure hadn't happened yet. And Louisa wasn't holding her breath. Folks from North Worcester played it pretty close to the vest.

"You want coffee?" he asked. That was his solution to everything. Flick's body must have been made up of three-quarters caffeine, the way the world was supposedly 70 percent water.

Louisa shook her head.

"Spill," he said, nudging her leg with his bony knee. "If you feel like it."

Louisa told him about the surprise in her mother's will. Flick didn't appear shocked, though his mouth dropped open for a second when she told him about the unknown brother. Then his face went back to looking calm and thoughtful. Mostly his dark gray-blue eyes were busy searching her eyes, trying to figure out how Louisa felt and what tack to take.

"Damn," Flick said in his slow, scratchy voice. "It's hard to wrap your brain around that. A son. Crap. I don't know. I mean"—he pushed his baseball cap back and rubbed his head, then straightened the cap again, adjusting the brim to be sure the sun didn't fall into his face—"we all have secrets, right? But that's a big one." He was speaking from firsthand experience. He'd been through it. Flick's first wife had turned out to be a drug addict. Mostly heroin, sometimes speedballs. After twelve years of marriage. His wife had been hiding it, shooting up in the bathroom, in the closet, wearing long sleeves in summer. He'd had no idea. So Flick knew what he was talking about, when it came to secrets.

"I don't believe it, though," said Louisa. "My mother? Seems like they're making it up."

"Yeah but that's exactly what I mean. I once dated a woman who had twenty cats. I didn't have a clue. —Jesus. I must have no sense of smell." He leaned forward. "—So. Louey-Lou. How you holding up?"

Louisa told him about falling apart in her lawyer's office, making a stinker of a scene, which made Flick chuckle. Then he reminded her of the time a bee flew through the window of their third-grade classroom and into her long hair and Louisa went running around the room, screaming like a maniac and flapping her arms, which she hadn't remembered till that minute, and that made *her* laugh, which felt a hell of a lot better than bawling. Then Flick started in on all other kids in class, including Constantin Spanos, who everyone had called Sparrow, how Sparrow had caught the bee gently in his cupped hands and then walked the bee down two flights of stairs, and outside into the schoolyard, where he released it. He was Dr. Spanos now, a popular local GP.

"You think anyone calls him Dr. Sparrow?" asked Louisa.

"I hope not," said Flick. "Ran into him at the Price Chopper a couple of weeks ago. He was looking good. His wife is still sick as shit."

Louisa flinched. Flick would say she was just a straitlaced Worcester Swede who still wore her skirts below her knees, but it wasn't that. Curses sounded out of place in Flick's mouth, like someone else was talking through him. Plenty of people in Wormtown were tough as hammers and talked like knuckle draggers—but not Flick. Louisa couldn't begin to explain why it bothered her so much.

Flick Bergstrom used to have a lousy reputation, years back. Dumber than mud, Flick would have said. Always getting into trouble. Then he'd add, bad choices make for interesting stories. He'd made plenty of bad choices so he had plenty of good stories. He'd raced dirt bikes and walked across the Wachusett Reservoir when the ice was razor thin. He was always wild and reckless. He took crazy chances. He'd drunk like a fish, dated the wrong girls, played in a loud garage band, committed a hundred foolish and illegal acts, and survived, just barely, that terrible Indigo Hill fire—but he wasn't a thug, not a bad guy. Not even close. Louisa's own breathing slowed, calmed down every time she was around Flick. Even her own husband didn't have that effect on her.

Suddenly Louisa felt like crying again, for no good reason. Stress, she guessed. Too much going on at work all of the time, case overload. She'd already canceled out her clients for the rest of the day, and Brandi, her office manager, would be pitching a fit. Social work was nothing more than a numbers game nowadays. You crammed in as many clients as you could. Instead of a front door, they should install a turnstile. With a slot to shove the money inside. Screw the clients, never mind the piles of paperwork. Just keep 'em coming.

We Are U.S. of A. served Worcester women and children at risk. That was an ever-growing population. It was sad to see. First the center was called Handicapped Children; then when that name became politically incorrect they changed the name to Families Valued, and when people thought that sounded like an antiabortion clinic they got this new, even stupider name. The staff held contests to see who could come up with the best worst names. We R Us. We Are Useless.

Rhonda, the WAUSA director, was not amused. She had about as much sense of humor as a bag of gravel. She and Brandi, the young pretty office manager, were what they called "besties." They were always going out together shopping at fancy boutiques in Shrewsbury and Natick, or out to lunch. They even went on vacations together. The rest of the staff called them the Beasties. You had to laugh—or you'd never stop crying.

Flick straightened and flexed his long fingers, to loosen them up. They looked more like a sensitive piano player's hands than a guy who talked about "a shit show" and dropped the f-bomb fifty times a day. The fire had left his joints as stiff as an old man's. He was on all kinds of pills and supplements. Flick had rheumatoid arthritis and he wasn't even forty-five years old. Wet weather and cold just made things worse, and it had sleeted earlier that morning. Flick was always standing up in the middle of a Gang of Six meal and stretching his limbs, shaking himself like he was trying to climb out of his own skeleton.

"You hurting?" Louisa asked.

Flick turned his hands over, staring at them front and back, gloomily. "It is what it is," he said.

At the moment there was no wedding band on Flick's left hand. He was in one of his unmarried phases—that's how Louisa thought of it, like a passing phase of the moon. An unattached Flick was rare. Flick usually had some woman or other hanging around his neck, claiming him. He declared he could take a hint, that two spectacularly failed marriages had proven he wasn't cut out to be anybody's husband. "I'm done with love," he vowed. His first wife, Trixie, was the one who turned out to be hooked on heavy drugs and his second wife, the Georgia Peach, whom none of the gang had ever met, had taken him for every nickel when she threw him out. No children either time.

It was a shame because Flick would have been a natural at the whole family thing. He would have been the kind of dad who played catch till after dark, taking his kids on camping trips, swimming with them, teaching them how to build and fix things. Louisa and Art, they'd never wanted kids. They had agreed on that way back when. Too much worry, not to mention the expense—look what her sister Michelle and Joe went through, agonizing over Sierra and her health problems. But Louisa was willing to bet Flick had always wanted a family of his own. Chances were wife number three would be some fertile blonde young enough to deliver. But even Flick was running out of time. He'd better get married again, soon. Or resign himself to living alone. He didn't seem to mind that. Louisa suspected that was one of the main things she and Flick had in common. Seemed like neither one of them was really cut out for full-time living with another human being.

As if he'd read her mind, Flick asked, "What did Art say about your mom's will?"

Louisa shook her head. "I haven't told him yet."

"Oh man." Flick rubbed the scarred side of his face hard and then winced. He could never remember that he'd been in that fire. Whereas it seemed like she, Louisa, could never forget it. "Your boy Artie just loves surprises."

"Yeah he does," said Louisa. They both snickered.

Then she shook her head again, sobering. Art took these things hard. He had no resilience these days. He had always adored his mother-in-law. He'd called her Mom; he thought she was flawless. His own mother had died when he was still a senior in high school. Art would feel betrayed by this latest revelation. Betrayed and maybe even scandalized. He wouldn't find anything funny about any of this. Not one single thing. "Jesus H.," she said, thinking about it.

"Look on the bright side," said Flick. "Now at least you have a brother."

"Oh *please*," Louisa said, rolling her eyes.

"Hey," he said. "Brothers can come in handy. I have two . . . I speak from experience."

"One sibling is plenty for me," said Louisa. "And this guy's not *family*. He's just getting something for nothing. We're not all going to start spending Thanksgiving and Christmas together."

"How do you know that?" said Flick.

Louisa cut him a sharp look, but Flick could stand up to it.

"Lou, you can't know for sure. Don't assume the worst. You haven't even met the man yet, have you?"

"No," said Louisa. "He lives in England. Someplace I've never even heard of. He'll probably fly over, pick up my mother's stuff, sell it, and then head straight home. We'll never see him again."

"But you don't know that," said Flick. "Maybe he'll turn out to be a great guy. Someone you're glad to know."

"Yeah, well, I'm making an educated guess," snarled Louisa. "He didn't bother to fly in for the funeral, did he?" Now that she thought about it, she felt aggrieved. He could at least have shown up at his own mother's funeral.

"Hmm." She watched Flick take this in. He stayed quiet a few minutes, his now greenish-blue eyes bright, mulling things over. "You said he only inherited what's inside of the house, right? Probably nothing much of value there."

"Probably not," Louisa agreed. The thought made her feel a little better. "It's full of old junk."

"Old stuff your mom inherited from your aunt Gritta, right?"

"Right." Her aunt Gritta was ten years older than Louisa's mother. She was the kind of woman who looked like she must have been born old. Old and angry. When her husband had died of a stroke, Gritta seemed to withdraw from the world completely. She lived on for another two decades but she never had another dinner party, never went on another vacation. In fact she seldom left her house. People might have said she'd died of a broken heart, but Louisa wasn't sure her aunt Gritta even *had* a heart. She was one tough old bird. She wasn't affectionate with any of them—not with her younger sister Alma, not with either of Alma's girls. She was always making them wash their hands before they touched any of her expensive, creepy things. She'd been a collector of weird antique items—dead-eyed dolls, lead glass candlesticks, Japanese inkwells, commemorative plates, Civil War bullets—basically she was a high-class hoarder.

"I'll bet most of Gritta's stuff is gone by now," said Louisa. "I don't know what all my mother kept. There were a few Hummel figurines down in the china cabinet."

"Those Hummels can be worth something."

"Michelle and I get first pick, at least," Louisa said, cheering up. "The will says we can keep any three items we want."

"There you go," said Flick. "Take the stove, the fridge, and—there wasn't a Porsche parked inside your mom's house, was there?"

"I wish." Louisa added defiantly, "But I'll tell you what. I *will* choose the three most expensive things."

She knew her sister Michelle would never talk or even think like that. Michelle would select something for purely sentimental reasons, like some old worn-out thimble her mother had used. But Michelle was married to a successful Jewish lawyer. She lived in a fancy house on the ritzy end of the West Side. Michelle worked part-time and puttered around the enormous house, with all her little hobbies and her yoga and her art. She could afford to be eccentric. Louisa blinked away angry tears. "It's not even that," she said. "This is not just about the money."

"I bet you wish you'd had more time," said Flick. He picked up Louisa's hand and held it between his two palms. There was something brotherly and natural in the gesture. The backs of both his hands were scarred and puckered so badly it looked like he was wearing gloves. "I'm so sorry, Lou," he said in his raspy voice. "Sorry it happened like this. It's a shit show." He bent over her hand like he was going to kiss it. But he didn't.

Then he added, "Look at me, just spreading the sunshine."

Grief welled up in Louisa like a tidal wave. Grief, and the strangeness of being comforted. It felt like she was drowning. She could hardly bear this much emotion stirred up together. Her beautiful mother gone forever, out of reach, with all her secrets still intact—and Louisa could not call her back now and ask any questions.

All this time her mom had been lying to all of them. Her gentle, wonderful mom with the childlike bright-blue eyes. Her honest face. Louisa remembered that moment in the kitchen when her mother had started to say—what would it have been, anyway? There was no door to the other side you could fling open and call through. Why hadn't she let her mother speak?

Hey, Ma! What did you want to tell us? A tear dropped onto the back of one Flick's rough hands. Still he didn't draw away from her. He wouldn't.

Louisa would have to be the one to let go, and so she did, pulling her hand away and standing up. "I don't even know who we just buried," she said.

CHAPTER FOUR

Art Wandowski was far more angry than upset at the revelation in his mother-in-law's will, as it turned out. He clamped his lips together so his chin seemed to disappear completely into his neck, like a turtle's, and then he locked himself inside his narrow paneled den for the night. He didn't take disappointment well. He was shocked by the news, yes, but even more than that, he felt cheated. Art and Louisa had been counting on a certain amount for their inheritance. There wasn't anything greedy about those calculations; they were both practical people. Now, with the annuity and everything inside the old house going to someone else, that sum had been reduced. And it was going to an absolute stranger, which made things that much worse.

But the next morning Art emerged from his little den triumphant. His potbelly preceded him. Louisa watched him walk toward her, his feet splayed, holding a sheet of paper. He didn't used to be so out of shape. She couldn't remember the last time he'd worked out, or even attempted to do anything remotely athletic. But he'd been busy all that night, anyway, working out a plan of action. Art wasn't lazy. He'd printed up a list of all the possible legal moves they could make to protect themselves. They could contest the will outright, or hire a legal mediator. They could raise the question of whether Mrs. Johansson had been under mental duress or even in the early stages of dementia when she crafted the terms of that will. Art always came through big time for things like this. If he hadn't stayed on, year after dull, grinding year at Sloane's Manufacturing, he would have been every bit as successful as Michelle's husband Joe; maybe he would even have gone into law.

But Art had an exaggerated sense of loyalty; he'd never abandon that job at Sloane's. "They'll have to carry me out feet first," he used to joke—Sloane's was the first place that had hired Art; down in the steamy boiler room when he first started out, then into Building 7 where the big press machines were kept; a hard-working teenager with little or no prospects, and careless parents who didn't believe in higher education.

Louisa drove Art's carefully crafted printed list over to Michelle's house to discuss their options. The white sheet of paper rode next to her on the seat like another passenger. Michelle lived in the poshest part of the West Side, on Lenox Street, smack in the middle of the large houses and sloping front lawns. Joe and Michelle had recently updated their enormous kitchen and two downstairs bathrooms, and added on an extra wing to serve as a rec room for Sierra—as if the sulky teenager didn't already have two or three of everything.

Michelle's house on Lenox was big, white, and sprawling, like something out of a movie set, with green shutters on the windows and green porch swings placed strategically along the cavernous front porch. The neighborhood wasn't as single toned as it had once been, but it was still full of Jews, the way the North Side, where they'd all grown up, remained full of Worcester Swedes.

Louisa presented Art's handiwork to her sister with a certain natural degree of pride. She wished Joe had been there, too, to study and admire Art's list of ideas, but it was Saturday morning and Joe was off at his temple somewhere. His whole family was religious.

Art had outlined all the legal arguments in detail, going through each bullet point systematically. He'd have made an excellent lawyer, Louisa thought. But Michelle just stared at the piece of paper blankly. It hung down from her hand, almost touching the tabletop.

"Art thinks we can definitely fight this," Louisa explained. "We can contest the terms of the will. Maybe Joe's law firm could represent us." Louisa didn't say that Joe should do the legal work pro bono, but she hoped it was understood. Joe always handled family legal problems for free. Even for distant cousins and nieces and nephews. And why shouldn't he? He made plenty. "I think we have a good case," added Louisa.

"But why would we fight this?" asked Michelle.

"So a stranger doesn't take what's ours." Louisa pointed at the piece of paper, as if the logic of it was embedded right into the object itself. Plain as the nose on your face, her father used to say. Michelle could picture Louisa adding that phrase next.

"But it *isn't* rightfully ours," protested Michelle. "Mom set things up this way on purpose. She reviewed the will with Mr. Enright three separate times. Remember how they told us that?"

"But how many times *didn't* she review the will?" Louisa asked triumphantly.

"Huh?" said Michelle.

"Maybe she meant to change it, but she just never got around to it. You know how forgetful Mom was. Look," said Louisa. "Why should some random guy walk off with our things? Someone we've never even met?"

"He's not some random guy, Louisa," said Michelle. "He's our half brother. He was Mom's firstborn child."

"He was an *accident*," said Louisa. "Obviously."

"Okay, maybe. Even so," argued Michelle. "Mom wanted things handled a certain way and she left clear instructions. We should respect her wishes. She's been more than generous to us, Lou. That's what I think," added Michelle in a quieter voice. She had been deferring to her big sister all her life. It felt strange to be arguing against her. "Besides, the household stuff on Ararat can't amount to much. What did Mom have, really? Beat-up furniture—she'd never let me buy her anything new. A collection of old movies, some out-of-date clothes and a few figurines."

"Flick says the Hummels could be worth some money," insisted Louisa. "That's not even the point. Doesn't any of this *bother* you? The fact that Mom had a whole secret life she kept from us? That we suddenly have to deal with this—this *intruder*, none of us even knew anything about?"

Michelle kept staring at her blankly, as if *Louisa* were the real stranger, not this brother who had fallen on them out of the blue.

Louisa glared back. "Doesn't it even bother you that you both have the same first *name*? Did you notice his name is Michael? *Michael, Michelle.* Get it?"

Michelle and Michael, yes she got it. That had definitely captured Michelle's attention right off the bat. It made her feel like she had a secret twin, a shadow-self she'd never known. But it seemed more interesting than troubling. Besides. "He actually goes by the name Tom," said Michelle.

"How would you know that?" demanded Louisa.

Michelle didn't answer right away. With Louisa, she always felt like she was walking on eggshells. She sat in her kitchen chair and smoothed Art's list in front of her with the palm of her hand, trying to buy some time.

Art had numbered all of his arguments, and had added letters for subarguments—1a) 1b) and so on. It occurred to Michelle that she had never particularly liked her brother-in-law, though she'd known Art practically all her life. It made her feel mean spirited. Somehow she never felt like she really got to know him any better over the years, either, nothing beyond a bland exterior. They'd never had a single real conversation about anything important . . . She traced figure eights around and around her kitchen table. The double loop figure was the sign for infinity. Michelle glanced at the phone hanging on the kitchen wall, willing it to ring. Her husband Joe would know what to say. Joe always knew what to say to people.

"Michelle?" insisted Louisa, her voice ominous. "How do you know about his name?"

Michelle had always been intimidated by her big sister. She didn't know why. She felt so much less vivid than her sister. Louisa had never been cruel to her, never bullied her—never shoved her downstairs like some siblings she knew about, never hit her or pushed her around at all, at least not physically.

"I called him," confessed Michelle. She'd needed an operator's help putting the overseas call through. There were so many extra numbers to dial! How long had it been since she'd actually spoken to a real live operator? Everything about this new brother was strange and new and a little bit thrilling.

Her sister scowled. "How did you even find him?" demanded Louisa. "Why didn't you tell me before? What the hell did he *say*?"

"Eddie Enright gave me the number. We didn't talk long."

"Did he sound like a crook?" said Louisa.

"I don't know what a crook sounds like," said Michelle. "He just sounded—you know, English."

"Oh he did, huh? What's that supposed to mean? It's easy to fake a British accent, you know. 'Ey there, mate. 'Ow's it going?" Louisa demonstrated.

"Why would he *fake* a British accent when he lives right there in England?" asked Michelle. "He sounded—I don't know. Normal. Distant."

"Distant, like he lives in a cave somewhere? Or distant, like an asshole who doesn't care that our mother just died."

"He sounded—fine, Louisa. A little formal. He sent those," Michelle said, waving a hand toward an immense vase of flowers. Louisa had somehow overlooked them, though now that Michelle pointed them out, they seemed like the single brightest and most remarkable thing in the room, towering over every other object. They looked expensive, Louisa noticed. And they also looked British, or what Louisa had always imagined might grow in a British cottage garden, with tall pink and white lupines and red roses and peonies. But in fact she, Louisa, was the real flower lover, just as her mother had been. It wasn't fair. She was the one who slaved away in the gardens all summer till dusk fell and it grew too dark to see.

"You can have them," Michelle added, as if reading Louisa's mind. "He said the flowers were for the whole family."

"You called him. So you guys are pals now. You two are buddies."

"I spoke to him once, Louisa. Briefly."

"Oh, this is bad," said Louisa, shaking her head, speaking mostly to herself. "This is seriously bad. This is really, really bad."

Sometimes Louisa reminded Michelle of their cranky old aunt Gritta, the collector. Holed up in that house alone with all her things. When Aunt Gritta didn't like something—which was all the time—she'd say it was bad. When she *really* didn't like something—which was still most of the time—it was bad, bad, bad. Sometimes an offense even got four *bads* in a row. Like now.

"I can't believe you talked to that man behind my back. This is so, so bad."

"His name is Tom," Michelle corrected her.

"Who cares!"

"Tom is our half brother," said Michelle. "Our mother's child. We share the same DNA. Doesn't that mean anything to you?"

"Yes," said Louisa, pulling the vase toward her and admiring the cut flowers in spite of herself. There were fragrant star lilies hidden in among the long-stem roses, and sweet-smelling freesia. "It means Mom was lying to us all these years. What else did she leave out? Was she a bank robber, too? Maybe she was a gang member."

"Oh Louisa," said Michelle. "Everyone makes mistakes when they're young. Didn't you? Ever?"

Louisa ignored this. She was thinking about what Flick had said: Everybody has secrets. Fair enough. But not all secrets hurt people. Some secrets spared people's feelings. That was a totally different thing.

Michelle tried again. Maybe a more positive approach would work. "Aren't you even a little glad that we have a brother somewhere out there in the world? Someone we never even knew about? It's like a little piece of Mom is still alive out there. Isn't that a good thing?"

"No . . . Not to me," said Louisa, turning the vase around slowly. "I don't need a brother. But *you* never felt like we were enough."

"What do you mean?" said Michelle.

"You spend half your holidays with Joe's family. You're always talking about how *great* they are. How *warm* they are." Louisa kept tracing the ridges on the cut-glass vase. The angles caught every color of the light, in tiny rainbows. The vase looked expensive, too, but maybe it belonged to Michelle.

"Well, they are," said Michelle. "That doesn't mean you're not."

"Ha," said Louisa gloomily. "We'll see. Now that Mom's gone. We'll see how much time you spend with *our* family."

"You're the one who never needed the family," said Michelle. "You've always had your stupid Bridge gang. There must be thirty of you from the old neighborhood, still getting together all the time. You're the one who still hangs out with your friends from kindergarten!"

A silence fell between them.

"So what exactly did you discuss with this—this person?" asked Louisa. She refused to call some stranger, a foreigner in fact, her brother. She had to draw the line somewhere.

"Logistics, mostly."

"Such as?"

"When he's planning to come see the contents of the house, what he's going to do while he's here, things like that," explained Michelle.

Louisa kept turning the vase slowly around. It seemed infinite. One side revealed spikes of bright-blue delphiniums. Her favorites. "And . . . ?" she asked.

"Well. He'd only just heard the news. He apologized for not coming to the funeral."

"Oh," said Louisa. "A little late."

"I think he's flying in to Boston, though. At some point soon." Michelle tried to make her voice chipper, like she was conveying some piece of unexpected good news.

Louisa didn't go for it. "He'd better come really soon. We need to put Mom's house on the market. This is the selling season, spring. We're not just going to wait around for him forever."

Michelle kept tracing her figure eights on the table, not looking up. "I explained all that."

"So I guess you're not going to help protect our legal interests after all," said Louisa, stiffly. She reached over, took back the piece of paper that Art had worked on so hard, folded it into quarters, and shoved it into the depths of her pocketbook. She'd have a tough time explaining all of this to Art.

"Tom said we could take anything we like from the house, Louie. We shouldn't feel limited to three items, either. He was actually quite—" She wanted to say *kind*, but that wasn't quite the right word, either. *Kind* implied someone warm and friendly. "Pleasant," she finished.

"Hmp," said Louisa, as if being pleasant was a deep and fatal flaw.

"Really," said Michelle. "I think you'll like him. If you give him a chance."

"I bet," said Louisa.

"I do think so. Really," Michelle repeated hopelessly.

Louisa folded her arms. All this time she'd been asking for a little support from her only living relative. And Michelle hadn't even offered her a cup of coffee. Not that she needed or wanted the coffee. But still, her sister might have offered. Or put out some cheese and crackers, like she would have done for one of her regular friends. "So now he's your best friend."

"I . . . No." Michelle wanted to say, Louisa *you're* my best friend, but it so obviously wasn't true. Her husband Joe was her best friend. After that came everyone else. Even Sierra came after Joe. But if she thought about pure friendship, between grown women, her older sister Louisa would still have landed pretty far down on the list. "I was thinking his coming here might help us," Michelle said instead.

"Yeah, right," said Louisa. She gave the vase another quarter turn. Hollyhocks, this time. Purple and pink. Could there be such a thing as too many flowers? This bouquet felt like somebody showing off, trying to prove a point. Big deal. So he spent a bundle on some expensive flowers. They'd all end up dead in the trash anyway.

Michelle spoke softly but clearly. "Did you want to have to clean out Mom's house yourself? It's going to be a lot of hard work. Messy work. And sad. Now he'll be responsible for getting rid of anything we don't want."

"True," said Louisa. The idea of this man having to pay for the movers cheered her up a little. And she was beginning to picture this large vase of flowers on her bedside table. No, in the living room where you could see it as soon as you walked in. No—the kitchen, where she spent the most time. It would be an enormous splash of color, a relief from all the beige and gray. But that was the trouble with cut flowers. They died quickly. They never lasted. That's why Art never bought them, he'd once explained. It was like just throwing good money away.

"Let me help Tom clean out the house," said Michelle. "Please, Lou. You've done the lion's share of the work for Mom this last year or two. You did the grocery shopping, and kept track of the bills. You drove her all over town. You're the one who took her to that awful doctor's appointment when she . . ." Michelle's voice trailed off. "When she . . . found out. The bad news." Michelle couldn't help it. Her voice got all choked up.

"Okay! Don't cry," said Louisa. It sounded more like an order than comforting, though she reached out and patted the hardwood table. "You had Sierra to look after. I have nobody." Three smart taps. "Stop sniffling. Quit it. You can take care of the house if you want. It's fine!"

"Thank you, Louisa," said Michelle. She felt so relieved she was almost giddy. She didn't even know why. Maybe everything would turn out all right after all. She grabbed a tissue from the box on the table and blew her nose. Now she'd have an excuse to go in and out of the old house on Ararat, at least for another few months. It seemed like a reprieve. Michelle had always loved the way the old house felt. Even the way it smelled. She could have gone away somewhere to college, but she couldn't bear to leave home, not even when she was eighteen. The bedrooms were tiny and filled to the brim, little more than walk-in closets. You could hardly turn around inside her mother's house. But she'd grown up there, looking at those close walls, those white ceilings, dreaming her childhood dreams. Sometimes she felt lost inside this large house on Lenox Street.

"Call Kim about the listing," Louisa ordered. Kim was married to Paco, one of the Gang of Six—another survivor of the fire. Paco had dragged Flick out of the burning shack on Indigo Hill. His wife Kim was a real estate agent in Worcester, and a successful one. "She knows what she's doing. She'll sell it fast."

Michelle hesitated. This was a bit delicate. "Are you sure you don't want to keep Mom's place for yourself?" she asked.

"What for?" said Louisa, surprised.

Michelle just shrugged. She'd always hated that little box of a ranch that Louisa and Art lived in. It felt like a shoebox, an empty imitation of a real house. Of course she couldn't say any of that aloud. She didn't want to offend Louisa.

Louisa narrowed her eyes at her sister. "I have a house," said Louisa.

"But all your friends still live in the old neighborhood."

"So?" said Louisa, staring at her. "What a weird idea."

Michelle shrugged. She couldn't explain why it felt like a good plan. Maybe she was just being selfish, wanting to keep the house in the family.

For just a minute, Louisa allowed herself to picture it. Moving back home to Ararat Street. The small bay window in front letting in all the southern light. The familiar backyard, sloping steeply uphill, the sky turning purplish-blue in summer, with the First Presbyterian Church spire in the distance. Everyone she knew living nearby. The two towering old chestnut trees in the backyard, which had somehow survived every blight and storm. The three straggly blueberry bushes by the back door putting out a handful of fruit. But Art would hate it there. He'd grown up in a dilapidated three-decker on the North Side, and couldn't wait to get out of the old neighborhood.

"No.—But thanks," Louisa added grudgingly.

The two sisters just stayed sitting for a minute or so, each lost in her own thoughts. They were so quiet they could hear the sound of the big chrome refrigerator humming.

"So what do you think he was like?" Michelle asked at last. "Do you ever think about that?"

Louisa scowled. "Tom? I have no idea. You're the one who talked to him, not me."

"No," said Michelle slowly. This was definitely dangerous territory and she wanted to be careful. "I didn't mean Tom . . . I meant—our brother's father."

"Who?" said Louisa blankly, then she flinched. "Oh," she said. "Him."

CHAPTER FIVE

That was just like her sister Michelle, thought Louisa, to make you brood about something you couldn't do a thing to fix. A fat lot of good it did. Her brother's father, that was putting it politely. The guy who'd knocked her mother up. Apparently he hadn't even stayed around for the birth. Now she couldn't get it out of her head, the injustice of it all. Some jerk out there was probably still alive in the world. Some *Englishman*. She figured whoever he was, he'd been her mother's first. At least she sure *hoped* he was the first. There were only so many surprises she could stand.

Alma had always made it sound like their father, Eric Johansson, was the absolutely utterly only man in her life, if not in fact the only man in the known universe. So who was this other guy, anyway? Was he still around? Alive and well, and never thinking twice about the American girl he'd once knocked up. As usual, the man walked away scot-free. It just wasn't fair. Louisa didn't want to spend a minute thinking about him, and now here she was, grinding her teeth over it. And there was nothing she could do to change it, or make it better. Trust Michelle to introduce a subject like that.

It was Saturday, but the Gang of Six (eight of them showed up that morning, in fact) had already met for breakfast. They'd chewed over the news of the will. Mostly Paco and Flick had made stupid jokes, but it still felt good to laugh. At least they could talk about it. The rest of the weekend yawned ahead of Louisa now, empty as a barn. It was too cold still to go outside and garden in the yard. Her hands would freeze in the cold earth. Art was holed up in his study as usual, with the door closed. The room wasn't much bigger than an oversize closet, but he spent most of his time in there alone with his computer and portable TV set. Art Wandowski was a man of many independent hobbies. He built model airplanes. He collected and restored antique toy trains. He had a ham radio too, and he spent hours on the thing talking to strangers, all of them men, while she sat in the kitchen, eating her meals alone.

Not that Louisa was complaining. Some married couples were joined at the hip like Siamese twins, and never even came up for air—she had never, ever wanted a marriage like that. Look at Michelle and Joe, practically cemented to one another. They jogged together every morning before work, wearing the same stupid-looking matching jogging outfits, belonged to the same book group and cooking club, and of course they both took Sierra to her endless rounds of doctor's appointments. They even still had a "date night" once a week, and they'd been married for twenty years for Pete's sake! What in the name of lemons did they dig up to talk about?

Though, come to think of it, Louisa still met up with her old North Side friends twice a week. Sometimes more. They had occasional feasts at the Manor, and barbecues and picnics down by the reservoir. They met up at concerts downtown. She'd known those same friends for almost forty years and they never ran out of things to say. Still. It wasn't the same as spending every waking and sleeping minute gazing into the same damn face. Louisa at least had some time and space to herself. And now here she was wasting it, squandering her precious free time, brooding about her mother's distant past.

Honestly, she'd never given her mother all that much thought. What was there to think about? Louisa loved both her parents. She'd had an okay childhood, all things considered. They weren't well off, but they certainly never went hungry. They never lacked anything important. Her parents were always there if you needed them—Louisa just couldn't remember ever needing them. She had always been independent. Her mom and dad had gone a little easier on Michelle, of course, given her fewer rules and later curfews, but that's what usually happened with second children, Louisa figured. Plus Michelle had been a bit of a Goody Two-Shoes, the obedient type. Good at school, good at sports, good at pretty much everything, and classically pretty to boot, with that head of golden curls. Strangers loved Michelle, they were always giving her things: free hair ribbons, an extra slice of cake. Once a store clerk gave little Michelle a free watch while Louisa looked on, disbelieving. Nice, polite Michelle, playing happily with her collection of Barbie dolls. Humming to herself. She didn't require much watching.

The way that families often divide into teams or pairs, she, Louisa, had relied on her sensible dad, while Michelle ran to her mother with every scrap of news, every little heartache. Louisa knew her mother had loved her just the same as she loved Michelle. It wasn't like her mom and dad played favorites. They just naturally fell into pairs, especially when they went on family vacations to Marblehead or Cape Cod. She and her dad would walk along the margin of the sea, skimming stones, gazing out east toward what her father always insisted was France, while Michelle and Alma sat on matching towels holding down the shore like bright twin paperweights.

Neither parent was terribly demonstrative with their affections. That just came with being a Worcester Swede. They'd give you a hug if they hadn't seen you for a while, but Louisa had colleagues at work who couldn't get off the phone with a parent or leave their own house without saying I love you, I love you too. Louisa knew she was loved all the time she was growing up. But now that she thought about it, there wasn't a lot more that she *did* know. She had heard the story of how her parents had met, of course; that was an old family favorite—at the Sloane's annual company picnic one Fourth of July. They'd both gone after the same exact slice of watermelon at the same exact time.

"He got the watermelon, but I got the best man in Worcester," her mother used to say proudly. It became a family saying, whenever you got the best of a deal. *He got the watermelon.*

Louisa didn't know much about the years before her parents had met and married. She'd never been all that curious about them, either. Her parents were not especially interesting. Both her mom and her dad had lived dull, uneventful lives—or at least that was what Louisa had always grown up believing. Alma Johansson (née Larsson) was the youngest of five children, the last straggler of the family. All of her older siblings had predeceased her. Three had moved back to Sweden. Alma's mother—her name had been Ingebolt—hung herself from a closet door when Alma was still in grammar school, leaving the father to raise five children alone. They'd gone through some tough times financially. Sometimes food had even been scarce. The mother's suicide was a taboo subject, and no one in the family ever talked about it. "She was sick," they said, never spelling out if they meant physically or mentally. Her grandfather didn't even keep a photo of his late wife in sight. He had never remarried.

The little house on Ararat Street originally belonged to him, back when they called the whole area Swedish Hill. He'd moved in close to all his Swedish neighbors, first by himself, then with his youngest daughter, Alma, and her husband Eric. The old man later gave them the deed to the house, but he stayed on living there in a tiny upstairs bedroom till the day he died. Did they like living there, all squashed together? Louisa had no clue. They never discussed it. Louisa remembered her maternal grandfather only vaguely. She was still a kid when he passed away. He was a tough old bird, with a famous sense of humor. But since he told all his jokes in Swedish, Louisa never knew if he was really funny or not. Her grandfather threw back a shot of rye every day of his life at five o'clock, but she'd never seen him drunk. He'd practically existed on Swedish food: hardtack and Thuringer, or sometimes pickled herring. He ate little, as if food was an indulgence.

Alma had always cooked your basic American fare—meatloaf, hamburgers, an occasional Sunday roast. She cooked the same four or five things in rotation, week after week. Boring. But the food was always filling. And she always made enough for leftovers. Their fridge was always full.

As for Louisa's father—he was quiet, neat, and precise. Louisa liked to think she took after him. Eric Johansson had excelled in mechanical drawing in high school, where he ran track, and won a few medals. He'd been a runner in the army—another experience he never spoke about. He had great handwriting, it looked like it had been printed by a machine. He had worked diligently, first for Sloane's, then for the Worcester county waterworks.

As far as what she knew about her mother—well, Alma had finished high school and then went off to live with family friends in Cornwall, England, in the fifties as a domestic helper—Alma's one big chance to see the world. She'd been hideously homesick at first, but she hung on. If she was all that homesick, Louisa had always wondered, why didn't she just come home? Now she knew. You didn't come home pregnant, not in the 1950s. So she'd hung on and stayed away. Two years, Louisa thought. It was a long time, really, but it had always seemed like a blip on the screen of her mother's life. Alma had spoken fondly about the British family she'd lived with, how they helped her get over "the rough patches." Years later, she still went into ecstasies over English scones and clotted Cornish cream, about something called Stargazy pie, a pastry made with fish, which sounded disgusting to the rest of them.

Alma had never talked much about her time abroad. Louisa knew her mother had taken the train up to the city and visited the London museums and famous cathedrals, walking everywhere because the roar of the Underground scared her. She talked less about her time along the south coast, except that the smell of the sea followed her everywhere.

There was one yellowing snapshot of Alma Larsson (her maiden name), standing on a hill in Cornwall, her long hair blowing across her wind-chapped cheeks. She was tall, and she wore heels. Even in the black-and-white photo you could tell that her hair was blonde, her coat made of some bright color. She looked brave and adventurous. Louisa could picture that young woman getting herself into trouble. She must have been scared to death—alone and far from home—with a belly growing steadily larger. But her mother had never talked about any of that. Not a word. Never even hinted at it. She seldom spoke about her past in any way. That was her generation, Louisa thought. Her parents' wild years took place in the domesticated fifties. They kept themselves and their feelings in the background, and took good care of their kids. But her mother, Louisa realized, hadn't taken good care of all her kids, exactly. She'd had to leave her only son behind.

It would be like her mom to keep track of that absent child somehow. When Alma Johansson's mind caught hold of something, it didn't let go. Like a dog with a bone, her father used to say. She could worry a small thing to death while letting the big ones slide. She used to fret over the flower arrangements at church, but show up in the pew wearing her own cardigan inside out. She'd fuss over the folding of napkins, leaving the kitchen floor unswept. She'd lose sight of the forest not just for the trees, but for the sake of a single leaf. Yet no one had a softer heart. She was stubborn and quiet and dedicated whenever she had a cause. She'd kept a small mountain of greeting cards on hand in her tiny house on Ararat Street and she was always sending get-well notes and sympathy cards to friends and neighbors and fellow churchgoers and relatives. Some of those cards must have gone overseas to this missing brother, Louisa now realized.

But the idea that there had actually ever been another man in her mom's life—well, Louisa's mind just shied away from all that. There had never, ever been another man in her mother's life. It simply wasn't possible. Alma Johansson was a devoted wife and mother. She did not flirt. She didn't even seem to notice other men. There had always been her father, simply Eric, the adored husband, Eric "the great love of my life," Alma called him, as if it were part of his name.

But now, with a twist in her stomach, Louisa considered a new possibility. Maybe her mother called Eric "the great love of her life" precisely because he wasn't the *only* love of her life, maybe not even the true one—simply the "great" love—the one that had lasted. Louisa knew that her parents had cared for one another. They didn't have to sit around holding hands all the time to prove how much. If one of them ever got sick, the other one fluttered around, trying to be helpful. Eric Johansson had been unexpectedly struck and killed in his new car just one week before their forty-fifth wedding anniversary, and Alma grieved for him deeply and truly for the rest of her life. Louisa sometimes thought her mother had never stood completely erect again after her husband died. Which still begged the question of the other man. Was he British? Older? Richer? More adventurous? Had he swept the young Alma off her feet?

That was her little sister Michelle all over, to poke and prod, and open a wound. She never could let well enough alone. She had always badgered Louisa with her endless kid-sister questions. Why can't I hang out at the bridge with your friends? What are you thinking, Louey? How about now? . . . *A penny for your thoughts*. Then *a nickel*, then *a dime*, and finally, pocketing the quarter, the teenage Louisa would say, "I'm thinking what a pain you are."

Anyone would have guessed that Michelle would be the one to go into counseling or social work, not Louisa—though no one ever would have said Louisa should be an elementary school reading teacher. For one thing, she wasn't a great reader. Louisa had no patience for anybody or anything outside of her workday. She was the kind of driver who leaned on her horn if the car ahead hesitated more than a split second at a traffic light that turned green. Even at the suicide corner at Kelley Square in downtown Worcester, she just blasted her horn and plowed on through. She hated the lines at the Price Chopper; half the time she checked herself out so she wouldn't get some dim-witted cashier slowing her down. Louisa knew all that about herself. Yet she had infinite patience with her clientele, special-needs teenagers and young adults before they aged out of the system. If anyone had called one of her kids dim witted, she'd have jumped all over them. Michelle used to tell her, "You're the softie in the family, Lou. And I'm the only one who knows it."

Louisa dealt with manic-depressives and ADD cases, kids in wheelchairs, runaways, spectrum teenagers with varying degrees of autism, teen pregnancies, mentally delayed clients, and a few schizophrenics—and more and more these days, kids with something called Oppositional Defiant Disorder. Fifteen years ago, Louisa would have said that was just a made-up name for bad behavior. But she saw those clients day after day, week after week—and these young people had a genuine medical condition. They couldn't do what you asked them to do, not to save their own lives. They could barely open the door and sit down in their chairs without making a stink. They simply couldn't go along and get along. They were like the worst of the baddest bad-ass Bridge, Sign, and Wall gang she'd grown up with, on steroids.

Her gang had once burned down a shack by accident. These new kids would have done it on purpose. Then they would have bragged about it, online. Filmed and posted it. The world was going crazy—and this new revelation about her own family was just further proof that it was spinning out wilder and faster. Somewhere out there on the planet was Alma Johansson's *firstborn* child—another thought that stung.

Louisa had *always* been the eldest child, their firstborn daughter, the sole responsible one. That was her role in the family. Okay, it wasn't much to brag about, but it was her one claim to fame. She'd saved her money, pinching pennies while Michelle squandered hers trying to find out what Louisa was thinking. She, Louisa, broke the barriers: smoked the first cigarettes, drank the first hard liquor, took responsibility on the rare occasions when their mother went away.

And actually—come to think of it, hadn't Alma once returned to England alone? Back when the girls were in elementary school? Had that really happened, or had Louisa only dreamed it? Hadn't Louisa planned out all the menus and cooked some of the meals for a few days, maybe even for a full week? Because she *was* the firstborn child, the mature, responsible one. But now she suddenly wasn't sure about anything. Suddenly she was relegated to the role of middle child. The trouble spot. She didn't like that one bit. Or, even creepier, the possibility that her mother had once been in love with some unknown, unnamed Englishman. Maybe he was something even weirder and more foreign than that. Maybe he had been Greek, or Romanian.

"He was just some guy who took advantage," declared Art, when Louisa brought the matter up. "Nothing more to say."

Louisa was sure he was right—Art was always right about these things. He was the one who brought things back down to earth. Still, his answer made her feel deflated somehow. What had she been hoping for, anyway? A great, thrilling love story? Not likely.

Well, at least she could talk it over again at the next Gang of Six breakfast. They'd be jawing about this one for months. Even if they didn't have any concrete ideas on how to change things, the gang always made her feel better about everything in general. In fact, they seldom told each other what to do. They didn't even make suggestions, most of the time. But nothing in life seemed quite real till they'd chewed it over together.

Sure enough, that next Saturday morning, Paco was already ensconced at the corner table at Lou Roc's, looking around. As usual, the place was hopping. Somebody always had to get to Lou Roc's early, to nail a table down. Sometimes Paco's wife Kim came along too, but mostly not. Saturday was a big workday for real estate agents Louisa and

Art were there at the diner—Art grudgingly, because he had a load of yard work to do around the house, he said—and Flick would be late, of course. Flick always showed up late, and out of breath as if he'd run there instead of driving his flatbed truck. Jean-Marie had just texted to say she was stuck in traffic. Twice a day, every day, Worcester became a parking lot on wheels. From seven to nine in the morning. Then again, from three to five thirty, without fail. Even on the weekends. Louisa texted her back.

"I can't believe you girls rely on those things," said Paco, nodding at the phone.

"I can't believe you don't have a cell phone yet," said Art. "You're living in the Stone Age."

"I don't need or want one," said Paco. "Don't want some electronic device always ringing in my pocket."

"Welcome to the twenty-first century," Art said, but he said it good-naturedly. Art and Paco had been best friends since the third grade. They still went on hunting and fishing trips every fall and spring. Now and again, a ball game in Boston.

That left Skunk, who was sure to show up sooner or later. He'd been a wicked pisser as a kid; he'd finally settled down and worked for the post office for the past eighteen years. Hard to picture him trudging door to door, with a sack of mail over his shoulder. He'd once been captain of the football team, hell on wheels. They almost all had nicknames, silly ones that stuck. Skunk was short for Sikunski. Paco had loved Mexican food as a kid. Jean-Marie was always just plain Jean-Marie. Louisa was Louey or Lou, or to Flick, she could be Louisa May, after the famous Alcott author for whom she had been named. Alma Johansson had been a great reader, and she'd loved *Little Women*. She tried to share that love of her favorite books with her girls—without much success.

"It could have been worse," Louisa would say. "I could have been named Pippi Longstocking."

Skunk finally arrived, with a season's worth of Tornadoes tickets to be divvied evenly among the gang. And then Flick sauntered through the door. "Anybody order for me?" he asked, looking straight at Louisa.

"What am I, your wife?" she said, a little more sharply than she'd intended. Flick rubbed his chin thoughtfully. Art looked uncomfortable. But, as usual, Paco turned it into a joke.

"You wish," Paco said. "You both wish." Then he turned to Art with a grin. "You *all* wish!" That made them laugh.

CHAPTER SIX

Tom Birch stood outside the United Airlines terminal in Logan International Airport, frowning out at the pouring rain. The rain seemed tropical and barbaric, as everything so far in the United States struck him as barbaric: American voices always seemed to be either barking or honking; people wore strange bright sloppy colors and none of them tucked in their shirts. None of them knew how to stand in line like a decent person. And then there was the waste everywhere you looked. Paper cups and paper plates and serviettes. Plastic bags by the handful. Plastic forks, spoons, even plastic *knives.* The entire country was apparently disposable.

Tom was accustomed to wet weather of course. Even wild thunderstorms. England was a rainy country and his southern corner of it along the shore was particularly damp and storm inclined. But in Cornwall the wind blew in moist veils, the rain pattered lightly and continuously. It didn't sluice down in buckets like this, obscuring his vision of the terminal, and the oversize cars and caravans racing heedlessly through puddles. He stepped back from the curb as yet another passing gas-guzzling car soaked him, but it didn't matter, he had worn sandals innocently expecting a warm summer's day (he had checked the Boston temperatures daily for a week) and his feet were already awash. He pulled his waterproof khaki-colored fishing hat from a front zip on his backpack and jammed it on his head—not that it would do much good against this onslaught. But it was his favorite hat and he felt marginally better wearing it.

Irritably he checked his flip phone for a third time—still no message from anyone here in the States. He was used to checking for texts from Claudia; nowadays he had to force himself not to look, not to expect them. This trip had all been an enormous mistake, obviously; a waste of time and resources and Tom Birch—he never went by his given name, Michael, though the name was printed on his passport—hated waste more than anything in the world. He hated to give away even a single minute. There were urgent problems to be solved, both small and large. Global warming, for instance. While he stood there faffing about, every single minute another hundred and fifty acres of rainforest fell under a bulldozer, an area larger in size than the Vatican City. Seas were steadily rising, parasites spreading. The future was assured, he knew, and it definitely didn't look good. Tom tapped his damp watch, and adjusted his backpack so the straps weren't digging in so hard against his shoulder blades.

Where were this strange American woman and her husband? She had sounded so *enthusiastic* over the phone, so insistent that Tom stay on with them at their house. He should have known better than to have trusted that kind of wild heraldic hospitality from a complete stranger.

Now he was stranded in Boston, Massachusetts, in this "barbaric yawp" of a country, in the midst of a tropical downpour. He could barely see two meters in front of his face. The rain showed no sign of easing. Then Tom remembered he had put his phone on airplane mode upon takeoff and had accidentally left it there.

Hastily he made the adjustments, and immediately five or six texts flashed across his screen, along with numerous missed calls and voicemail messages, all from the same +01 American phone number. He flushed with annoyance. He had no time to listen to all the voice mails, but he hastily texted the woman, *Michelle. Apologies. Standing outside Terminal B, United. My error. T.*

As if she'd been standing staring at the phone, three dots began to jiggle up and down and she replied, *So happy! On our way!!! Xox Michelle.*

He had never seen so many exclamation points in one place, nor had he ever been the recipient of *x*'s and *o*'s. It gave him the strange feeling that his phone was no longer entirely his own. He retreated toward the wall of the terminal where, if he wouldn't have time to dry off, at least he wasn't likely to get any wetter. He traced the sound of planes overhead, but there were no white contrails, no vortices of airflow visible. You could barely make out the sky at all, so blocked was it by cloud cover and crisscrossing telephone wires and ugly airport buildings. The rain had a pulsing rhythm all its own. Five minutes passed. Then ten. More acres of rain forest fell. Another text arrived. *Help! Where are you? We can't find you!!! What are you looking at?*

He felt like typing back, *I'm looking at the rain, you idiot.* Instead he gave the terminal number. A white limo, long as an omnibus and emitting fumes, had pulled up and parked next to the **No Parking** sign, ignoring the sign with typical American arrogance. The oversize Cadillac appeared to be parked for the duration. The windows were blacked out, but a vibrating bass played so loudly within it made Tom's heartbeat twitch in syncopation.

Again the three dots on his phone jiggled up and down, up and down, like tossing waves. This went on for a minute or two, but instead of the long treatise he expected the woman wrote simply, *Oh!! Be right there!!!!*

Tom began to shiver. He doubted he'd ever been this wet standing outside an actual shower in a bathroom. He had checked no baggage in order to save on time and expenses, and because he believed in the virtues of traveling light. He wished now he'd insisted on staying at a hotel. Then at least he could count on a good hot bath, maybe a cup of tea, and a few hours of peaceful anonymous silence in his long day.

He felt the woman coming toward him from behind a minute or two before she spoke.

"Tom? Is it you?" asked a tremulous voice, and he turned to face an attractive blonde woman, just his height. If he'd expected some physical family resemblance, he detected none. Perhaps, if anything, the bright, almost electric shade of her blue eyes.

"Why, yes," he said, and hadn't had time to poke out his hand for a handshake when she enveloped him in a full-on embrace, taking in his soaking clothes and all, and then, to make things worse, actually rocked him back and forth in her arms as if he were an infant.

He broke free as soon as he decently could, and stepped back. A tall lean man stood waiting behind the blonde. At least he didn't attempt any full-body contact, just put out one long hand saying, "Sorry it took so long."

"We tried to meet you at the gate," the woman explained breathlessly. "But the way security is these days, ever since 9/11 . . ." She shook her head. "Well, at least we're together now. At last! Here." She thrust something into his hand. "These are for you!"

It was a bunch of daisies. Of course. Claudia's favorites. But these had been dyed or dipped, he supposed, and they were a frenzy of fluorescent colors: electric blue, shocking pink, barely flowers at all. They almost hurt his eyes. "Thanks," he said. "Too kind."

"We're just so *happy* that you're finally here," said the woman. "Oh, I can't believe this is really happening. I'm Michelle, of course." Mercifully she didn't say anything about being his long-lost sister. "—And this is Joe. Our daughter Sierra is in the car, plugged into something or other. Teenagers!"

"Right," said Tom. "Shall we push on then?"

After a certain amount of back and forth and after-you-ing and arguing over who would ride in the front seat—Tom insisted he'd be fine in the back—he crawled into an oversize American sedan, next to a girl who barely glanced at him, her eyes black-rimmed with kohl, her hair black as jet, her face round as a moon and almost as pale, with an unhealthy sheen to it. She looked bored almost to the brink of death. Her pallor reminded him for an instant of Claudia toward the end. He fought the unexpected pang at his heart, a claw. That was the tricky bit, he knew. You could never tell when another wave might rise up in that sea of grief and knock you off your feet.

"Hullo," he said to the girl. "I'm Tom."

She mumbled a few words. There was something wrong with the girl. It was hard to tell exactly what it was. Her lips were chapped, her eyes looked glassy—what little he could see of them behind a shock of greasy black hair. Perhaps she'd recently been ill. Another stab of pain.

"Sierra is sixteen," said Michelle, as if that explained everything. Possibly it did. Tom could not really remember his teens. The past was a blur. He was more than fifty now. He thought he'd probably been an ass; most teenage boys were.

"Pleased to meet you," said Tom. The girl gave him the barest glance, just grazing her eyes over him for an instant, then resumed staring out the window, licking her chapped lips. She wore some hair product that smelled like strawberries, only sweeter, and more artificial.

They pulled out onto the crowded three-lane motorway, which the blonde woman called "The Pike." She twisted almost completely around in the front passenger seat to smile at him. It gave him an odd sensation, since she was sitting on the wrong side of the car, from his point of view.

"So, I never asked you," she said brightly. "What is it you do exactly, for a living?"

"I'm a consultant." He looked down at his hands, folded in his lap.

"Really," she said. "Isn't that fascinating! What kind of consulting do you do?"

"This and that, yeah," said Tom.

The girl beside him snickered.

"Computers, chiefly," he added. His work was too complicated to describe or explain. Most of it was highly technical. Dull as ditch water.

If he mentioned the research work he did for the British secret service, they'd all assume he was a spy, which of course he was not. Nothing as glamorous as that.

"And what do you think of our president?" the woman went on, still awkwardly twisted around in her seat. Her neck must hurt, Tom thought.

"Seems all right," said Tom. He was not keen on politics.

"He's black, you know," she said, unnecessarily. "And this is his second term. We're all very proud of him!"

"For being black?" asked the daughter. "Would you be proud of him for being white?"

"Good point," chuckled the father. He seemed like a quiet, easy-going sort of person. He drove the large, crowded motorway with confidence.

"Oh, for Peter's sake," said the mother. "I just mean our country is making some strides. Finally. We'll never go back to where we once were, and I say good riddance! Next election we'll probably get a female president."

"Ha," said the girl. "Fat chance."

Tom looked at her.

"Let's try not to argue in front of strangers," said the father.

"No worries," said Tom.

"Except Tom's not a stranger," the mother put in quickly. "He's family!—But you mark my words about a woman president," said the mother. "And about time. It's only taken us two hundred years to get there."

"I take it you didn't like President Bush?" asked Tom.

"Oh!" Michelle looked distressed. "Oh, golly—I wasn't thinking . . . I'm so sorry! I forget you're not ever supposed to talk about politics. Did you Europeans all like George W. Bush?"

"I wouldn't presume to say." Tom realized he had somehow been thrust into the role of diplomat, spokesman, and family mediator.

Apparently he was now also the representative of an entire continent. It was dizzying, and he was still suffering from jet lag. Nor had he been fed a decent meal on the plane. Tinned beans and eggs. It had been billed as "an authentic English breakfast." He didn't know anyone in England who ate that poorly. As far as he was concerned, it was hours past his bedtime. He stifled a yawn. He went to bed early and rose early. "Obama seems all right."

"I'm so glad!" the woman enthused, her relief as visibly keen as if the president were an extended member of her own family. Perhaps he was, for all Tom knew. He knew nothing about any of these people, after all. Another dismal wave of loneliness rolled over him. Without Claudia, he was adrift in the world. He would be a stranger from now on, no matter what might happen, no matter where he might go. The day he'd buried Claudia, the sun had dropped straight out of the sky, and yet somehow daylight came, day after tiresome day.

"What year are you in?" he asked the girl, struggling for something to say. The sort of aimless adult question he had always hated, when young.

She didn't even bother to turn her pale puffy face toward him. He couldn't blame her. The rain had let up slightly, or perhaps they were driving through the soaked hills and valleys into a new microclimate. The names of towns flashed past, making it feel as if he was back in England: Brighton, Framingham. He knew Framlingham, a smallish town in Suffolk: Mary Tudor was proclaimed queen behind the stone walls of Framlingham Castle.

"I'm sixteen," said the girl in a barely audible voice. The register of her voice was deeper than he expected, almost an octave lower than her mother's.

"Tom means what year are you in school," said Michelle. "Sierra is in tenth grade," she announced. "We call it being a sophomore!"

"I call it being in hell," said the girl.

"As bad as all that?" asked Tom, hoping he'd trick her into looking at him. It was discomfiting, sitting next to a child who refused even to meet your eyes. It made him feel untrustworthy. He could see her ghostly complexion reflected in the car's side window, clotted by silvery drops of rain.

"Sierra was an honors student," said Joe.

"High honors," added Michelle proudly.

"Not anymore!" piped the girl. "Now I'm not smart enough even for low honors. Not here in Wormtown—that's what we call Worcester."

"I hate that name. I never call it Wormtown," said the woman.

"Wormtown is what it is," said the girl.

To Tom's relief the woman turned on the car radio. It played some mindless upbeat American pop song, about "call me maybe." Did that mean the person's nickname was Maybe? Tom couldn't make any sense of it at all.

Out the window Tom saw nothing of interest but the lashing rain; nothing else that drew him in, at any rate. If he could have made out the outlines of the mountains, that would have been all right, watching for where the high oaks gave way to maples and ash. In England the motorway ran right up along the margins of fields and farms. Cows and sheep ambled down onto the shoulders of the road, and now and again right across it. Here in America the green living world seemed a vast distance away, like something from a film. They drove in a center lane, which only made matters worse. Around them were nothing but cars and more cars. All of them so unattractive and alike it seemed as if they must have been designed to be ugly on purpose. Bumpers, fenders, and headlamps. Old bangers and articulated lorries. When finally he spotted a field of cows they were so distant they looked like the plastic figures in a child's play set.

After they'd traveled in silence another ten kilometers the rain eased up a bit, and the day turned gray as gristle. They passed factories, industrial complexes, and shopping malls. It was as if they had evaded nature entirely; stretch after stretch of carriageway whipped by, ugly and man made. For an instant Tom thought of snapping a photo to send to Claudia as proof that something this insane actually existed, and then he again remembered her absence with a renewed jolt. How long must this go on?

In any event, there was nothing around here that would have delighted even Claudia. She could find beauty in almost anything. Not here. The rigid backs of factories and blind windows of flats. Scrubby oaks; no hedgerows to speak of; no flowers at all, except, high on a hill, a patch of identical yellow flowers that thickly spelled out a single banal phrase: **Nice 'n Easy.**

Tom leaned forward and pointed toward the hill. "Is that the name of the town?" he asked. "Nice 'n Easy?"

Michelle chuckled. "It's a business," she said. "Farther west along the Pike you'd also find Friendly's, in Wilbraham."

"There's Liberty Mutual in Boston," Joe put in. "Peace in Dedham. Converse in Malden."

"And there's B.J.s in Natick," said the girl from her corner. "We all know what *that* means, right?"

Tom looked at her blankly for a few seconds before he got it. He hadn't heard those initials in a long time. Blow job. He really *had* been an ass as a teenage boy.

"Sierra!" scolded the mother. "Honestly."

The radio had moved on to a song about "the one that got away."

"It's quite a long journey from the airport," said Tom, shifting around uncomfortably. He was aware that the bottoms of his trousers were dripping water onto the carpet of the car. He wiggled his wet toes inside his sandals. Claudia had bought them for him. "You didn't need to collect me. I could easily have taken the coach."

"Just another fifteen minutes or so," the man reassured him. "You're not feeling carsick are you?"

The girl eyed him and inched away.

"Of course not," Tom said.

"We wouldn't have dreamed of letting you take a bus," said Michelle. "The very idea! We've all been so excited to meet you! I could hardly sleep a wink last night. And of course," she added, "you know you'll also see my sister Louisa tonight at our dinner."

There was something in her voice that sounded like a warning. "I take it she's not been dying to see me?" said Tom.

"Of course she has!" protested Michelle. "Louisa is—" She hesitated, apparently at a loss for words, for a change. "Louisa is different. She is her own person," she finished lamely.

"Amen to that," said Joe behind the wheel.

"Aunt Louisa is a weirdo," said the girl, Sierra. "And there's like something definitely wrong with Uncle Art."

"Now, that is enough of that!" exclaimed Michelle, putting an end to the conversation.

"I've recently had a loss myself," said Tom abruptly.

If you had wagered him a thousand pounds, he'd never have believed himself making unwarranted confessions to strangers. Less than an hour after he had first laid eyes on them, no less. Being in a foreign country felt oddly liberating, he was finding. Nothing here on this foreign continent seemed real. The lettuce-green American dollars looked like something you'd use in a child's board game. The coins were flimsy and light-weight.

"What happened?" asked the girl, Sierra. Her heavyset face was flushed for the moment, as if from the effort of asking a direct question.

"My—girlfriend, died," he said. The words sounded so lame. The concept of a "girlfriend" fell so unbelievably far short of what Claudia had actually meant to him.

"Oh! I'm very sorry," said Michelle, twisting around again to look at him. "You poor man."

"Bummer," said the girl. "Serious bummer."

"When did she pass away?" asked Joe.

"Seven months ago," said Tom.

"Oh my goodness," said Michelle. "That must have been a terrible shock."

"She'd been ill a long time." Hideously, tears came to Tom's eyes. He blinked them away and turned his head to look out the side window. "She died of MS."

Michelle faced front again. "But she couldn't have been very old, even so. My goodness!"

"Forty-one."

"That's how old I am!" Michelle exclaimed. Everything seemed to amaze her. She spoke only in exclamation points. "I'm so sorry! MS. What a terrible loss!"

"Well, you've had your own loss as well," Tom said. "Of course." Now he was feeling guilty as well as foolish. He should have voiced his condolences earlier. He had been an ass as a teenage boy, he was even more of an ass now. This woman had just recently lost her own mother. Would he ever outgrow his own stupidity? Apparently not. "With the death of your—um." Was he supposed to say *our mother*? He could not force those words out of his mouth.

"Yes, Mom's death was quite a heavy blow," she said.

"Everyone loved Alma," Joe put in. After a moment Michelle blew her nose. They drove along another kilometer or two. Then the teenager spoke.

"I don't see the point of living," said Sierra. "Everyone ends up old and decrepit, or dying. It's all so useless. I mean. What. Is. The point." She sounded like she might cry. "Seriously!"

There was a moment's total silence in the car. The radio was playing "Set Fire to the Rain." Adele's voice wailed. Joe reached out and switched over to a news station. The newscaster talked unbelievably fast. To Tom it sounded more like gibberish than the English language. He wished Claudia were there to translate. Something about a collapse of the mortgage industry. Maybe the announcer was trying to get the bad news over with.

After a moment, Michelle said faintly, "Well my goodness, Sierra." She didn't turn around in her seat again, but everything in her posture radiated worry and disappointment—the slump of her shoulders, the stiff set of her neck. Even her bobbed blonde hair looked sad, the pale ends curving under.

"Hey. Sorry," said the girl in a soft voice, touching her mother's shoulder. She glanced at Tom. "Sorry."

Tom gaped at her. Why should the girl apologize? He couldn't think of a single good argument for living at the moment, but neither did he want to say straight out, I quite agree with you. Let's just make a sharp turn into the next tree and end it all. Instead he offered the black-haired girl a wrapped stick of Doublemint gum.

"Can't," she said. "But thanks."

"Sierra needs slow-acting carbs," explained her mother. "We watch her numbers like a hawk. She has type 1 diabetes. You might find that's the topic of quite a few of our conversations," she added.

"Or all of them," said Sierra. She offered up a singular grin.

~

Dinner that night at Michelle's house was a lengthy, knock-down, drag-out affair that went on for hours. Tom hadn't sat in one place that long in years. Nor was his chair especially comfortable. There was far too much food, all of it too salty, and everything, even the salad, tasted greasy or fried. The vegetables were limp and heavily sauced. The wine was bad, and came in enormous bottles.

Granted, the British were a circumspect lot, never the type to air their dirty laundry, but did he really need to be introduced to the whole world as a newly found relation, given his unorthodox role? "I'm the bastard," he was tempted to say. "How do you do?"

~

All night long he was prodded to tell his story over and over—and really, there wasn't much to say. "His biological father is dead!" one sister called to the other, unmistakable glee in her voice. What on earth was wrong with these bloody people?

Neighbors and friends as well as acquaintances seemed to come and go at will, carrying on, milling about aimlessly, and after a few hours Tom could no longer remember which of these people he was supposedly related to. By the sixth or seventh introduction, he gave up and confessed himself lost.

"But you do remember *us* at least," chided Sierra, circling a black-lacquered fingernail toward herself, her mother (Michelle), and her father (Joe).

"Yes," Tom reassured her. "I know who you are."

She sank back in her seat. "Well, that's all that matters," she said. "We're the fun ones."

"And we are the broken ones," quipped the older sister, Louisa, from across the table. It was the first time she had volunteered a full sentence all night.

She sat beside a sulky, feminine-looking man who refused to look at Tom. Not directly, at any rate. Nor had he spoken a word. Not even a hello. Why?

The older sister's unexpected phrase, *the broken ones*, captured Tom's attention. It actually made him catch his breath.

He knew what Claudia would have said. She'd have said that Tom was attracted to brokenness like a fly was to honey. And she'd have been absolutely right. It was his need to fix things. Solve mysteries. To pluck the invisible web of connections, and draw the lines taut between them, putting the world to rights. Suddenly he felt alive, alert. He looked more closely at the tall, gaunt woman, Louisa, sitting across the dining room table from him. She was the elder of the two sisters, he believed.

Her hair was drawn tightly back from her face, as if to keep the bones pulled together. If she didn't look so fierce, she might have been an attractive woman. Her body was athletic looking, energetic. Her husband—Tom forgot the man's name—leaned his whole pudgy body away from the table, looked away. Even his feet pointed away, toward the door. Everything proclaimed that he was not really in this room, and that he preferred to be elsewhere. Now and again Tom felt the man sneaking a glance at him, and it reminded him of a predator in the wild. Tom had known enough unhappy couples to recognize the symptoms of a stale marriage. But the trouble here seemed to go deeper. There were sharp lines carved deeply on either side of the woman's mouth.

Ah, Tommy, he seemed to hear Claudia say. *Don't go poking around where you're not wanted.*

"You don't have to look so serious," said the gaunt woman, Louisa. "I wasn't asking you to fix us."

"But that's what I do," Tom said seriously.

They all laughed. Even Tom managed to crack a smile.

Now you're in trouble, said Claudia. She sounded pleased as punch.

CHAPTER SEVEN

This new person, Michelle, suddenly plunged into his life, was an eager and early riser. Back at home, in his own time zone, Tom rose early too. In fact he seldom slept past 5:00 a.m., the deep-blue moment when the shimmering margins of damp earth and sky began to blur, as if sending advance notification of a sun about to rise. Insects stirred, leaf stems quivered. The whole shivering world fairly vibrated with life. That was his favorite hour of the day, for thinking and for tracking.

But here in the States Tom slept like the dead and woke unrefreshed. He had moved into one of those faceless, soulless American motels on the outskirts of Worcester at his first opportunity. There was nowhere to walk, and apparently nothing worth walking to. His mattress was thick and soft as a loaf of bread. Michelle and Joe had insisted he was no trouble at all, that he was a welcome guest—and even the girl Sierra protested against his going—but Tom could no sooner sleep in a house full of strangers than hang in a tree suspended inside a spider's web. The motel was faceless, comfortingly anonymous, almost miraculously without character. Unattended, he'd have slept like the dead, hour after hour.

He hadn't yet needed a motel wake-up call; Michelle provided that service. Tom was still on Cornish time. He missed the salt tang of the sea. His long habit had been to rise at four or four thirty, when the world fell still, unprovoked even by light; the blurred hour, he had learned, when people in hospitals were most likely to turn over in their hospital beds and die. Things happened at the border places. Back at home, Tom would rise from the bed, careful not to disturb Claudia, and silently would tidy up the kitchen, and plump the kettle for Claudia, who wouldn't wake till after seven. He had never used those first solitary, silent hours for business, it would have seemed to him a sacrilegious waste of time.

Tom treated the early morning, he imagined, the way his Protestant ancestors used to preserve a Sabbath. In his case, it had nothing to do with prayer or churches. The solemn hour before dawn was silence and being open to that emptiness. It was for Tom a time for close and uninterrupted observation, not an opportunity to be taken lightly. He crept out into the dew-drenched furze like someone sneaking out to a lover. Birds ruffled their feathers and revealed themselves on the branches of trees. Clouds scaled the blue-gray sky and formed fantastical shapes. Leaves visibly uncurled, or trembled in a rain-bearing wind. Worms crowned through their beds of dirt, writhed and spun about and headed through the roots of grass. If you held still for even one full minute you could detect signs of life in all directions. Of course, most people found it unbearable to hold still for more than a few seconds.

If Tom had been a believer, this hour would have been his religion. In the brief moments before dawn broke, the inky-blue world and all its mysteries lay half-open, like a blooming rose, and on close inspection revealed some of its secrets. Some, but never all. The mystery kept it fresh. Research was his avocation, how he made his living, but this, the tracking out of doors, was his real work.

Tom was a tracker by instruction and inclination, as was his father, and his paternal grandfather and quite likely his great-great-great grandfather before, going all the way back till all his ancestors swung out of the trees and began walking without leaning on their knuckles, looking around. He was related to them not by blood and birth but by a shared curiosity. The exact right family had adopted him. He knew that his biological father had passed before he was born, a fallen soldier in a forgotten war; his biological mother, a strange American, sent birthday and holiday cards and occasional strange gifts that meant nothing to him. Other people were indifferent to this world, blind to it, and he could not comprehend such people at all.

His was not a profession, but a calling; trackers were people who closely followed the trails of living things. For some, like his da, that meant tracking animals. For others, it might mean tracing the path of the wind, or watching to see what had broken the twigs off a rowan bush. "Evidence of things unseen," the Bible said. But for Tom, it was the evidence of things unattended that drew him on. The great trick, perhaps the only trick, was to pay attention as if the world around you actually mattered.

His father had always been better at stalking than at tracking, the difference being a question of what appealed to you most. His da was a nutter about animals. He and Claudia would have gotten along like twins, but his da was long gone. A stalker was only after the living presence—usually an animal of one kind or another, moving about. A tracker was someone who stood at the center of a mystery and tried to ferret out where all of the radial lines converged. The wind, the grass, the sleet, the winding river all connect at the root. But his father had loved only the animals. All animals had fascinated him equally, large or small, domestic or wild, without preference to reptile, amphibian, or mammal. His da was as interested in a field rat as in a diving winnard, and small hovering insects intrigued him as much as a fin whale speeding off the shore of Land's End. He wasn't so good with people. Likely that's why his father drank, night after night; not a sloppy falling-down drunk, but stiff with it, the glass rigid in his hand. Then when daylight came, he had seemed sober as a judge.

Tom was not really focused enough for stalking animals; his mind tended to wander. His paternal grandfather, however, now he was the past master at both stalking and tracking, and he had taught Tom everything he knew, and everything worth knowing. The old man recognized and could recreate every nuance of every birdcall; he could twist ordinary thin dogbane growing in a field into a rope strong enough to tow a car; the old man read the palest stars by daylight; he came and went as freely as one of the sea birds. His senses had never missed the smell of lightning, or a bent blade of grass. His grandfather was the kind of tracker who could slip in and out of sight while you stood there gawping at him. And if the old man wanted to sneak up on you, just to prove that you weren't paying the proper attention, well, you didn't stand a chance against him.

None of Tom's family had been avid hunters; they went out into the wild for the sake of being out. Simple enough. You either loved it or you didn't. It wasn't something you could teach someone to care about—so he counted himself lucky to have been adopted into this particular bunch. It could easily have been otherwise. Tom supposed the hunger for this kind of knowledge was something you were born with. Claudia had enjoyed a long ramble, but she had no patience for tracing the claw prints of a stick insect or measuring the movement of a falling wind.

They'd had no children together, not for lack of trying. Perhaps Claudia had been sick for longer than either of them realized. So—no heirs. The knowledge and the skills Tom had spent his life acquiring would die with him. These days you didn't find many fellow trackers, anyway. Tracking was old school and slow. Not for the trendy. Everywhere you took a step now into the fresh air, you encountered a mob of noisy outdoorsmen, elaborately outfitted and weighed down with expensive toys. They were all robust and poshly dressed in overpriced flannels and intent on improving their massively good health—hikers and joggers and yoga experts and the like.

To track cost you nothing but time and energy, though it was hugely demanding of both, and that made it less interesting to the upwardly mobile. You went out into the fields, you looked around. You paid attention, that was all. Tracking required silence and focus, two things in short supply even in Tom's quiet, out-of-the-way pocket of Cornwall. And here he was now, half a world away, stranded alone in a sea of tar and concrete.

Tom hadn't done any tracking in America, he'd barely gone out for a decent walk, whilst back in Cornwall he regularly covered between ten and fifteen kilometers a day. His best thoughts always came to him on his feet, moving. But here in America he had no thoughts. He holed up in his motel room, waiting supine for the next thing to overtake him. Gasping for air, the proverbial fish out of water, waiting for it to come clear why he had flown across the ocean in the first place. There he lay, destroying the hours, rumped up like a winnard.

I am in mourning for my life, Claudia teased him, in a thick Russian accent. Probably quoting Chekhov or Turgenev. Oh, she had been a grand reader. Tom never saw a single person reading a book in America, not even a used paperback or a tattered magazine. People were too fixated on their gadgets, staring into screens. Now Tom was becoming like them.

It was his third wasted morning in Worcester and they were finally getting down to business—or so Michelle promised him. The first day of Tom's arrival something had come up about the girl Sierra's health—she had diabetes, Tom quickly learned, of a particularly troubling type. They'd needed to drive her to the doctor's office to adjust her glucose levels after noticing that she had moderate to high ketones. Michelle spoke in these technical terms, as if Tom were a fellow medic and together they could solve whatever ailed the girl. Only Tom didn't know what really ailed Sierra. Something more than the diabetes, certainly. He understood the rudimentary facts of blood sugar; he even knew the basic difference between slow and fast carbs, but he didn't know what made this girl dress like a pauper, why she crept around the posh house in black rags, looking like death itself. He recognized the symptoms of despondence, but could not lay his finger on its cause.

His second day in the States, Michelle had been called in to work at her school. She invited Tom along—"I'll introduce you to everyone!" she announced. "They're all dying to meet you. Really and truly. Especially the kids!"

Tom was certain he had nothing to offer a roomful of eager schoolchildren; Claudia had been the one who had a way with kids. Once a complete stranger, a little toddler with black eyes, had run straight into her arms at a public park. These days Tom could not even reliably crank out a smile, so he stayed back at the motel, and caught up on office work on his laptop, took care of a few more of the endless ghastly details that accompany a death. Perhaps the red tape was set out deliberately to distract the bereaved, he mused. Because Claudia had been sick so long, and because they'd never married, scofflaws that they were, distrustful of legal contracts, the paperwork left behind was an especially gnarled tangle. He wished now that they'd married. But it also gave him comfort—even if it was a false comfort, Tom was grateful—that even now, months after Claudia's death, he might continue to serve her in some small way.

He still hoped to get into the city of Boston sometime and poke around in some of the famous public gardens and parks. Perhaps he would visit a museum or two. He had barely a passing interest in collecting this family inheritance. He'd done nothing to earn it. Nor did he lack for anything. The mystery, really, was why he had come to the States at all, when he might have spent the airfare on a trip to the Canary Islands, as his few mates had suggested back home. He wasn't one to dwell on family connections. He always knew his biological mother existed somewhere out in the world and he knew his father had departed before he'd even been born. None of that had ever interested him. So what had pulled him across the ocean now, fifty years later? Morbid curiosity? A search for missing threads of his DNA? But he'd never wondered about his birth parents, he knew what had happened to them; he took it as a sign that he'd landed where he had. The right couple had adopted him. He'd known that from the start. He was in the right place, doing what he was meant to do. Or so he had felt for a long time. As long as he'd had Claudia it seemed he had everything he could possibly need. Now that too was over.

If he had hoped to forget Claudia's absence here in America, to put her frail ghost to rest, he had failed miserably. Even the motel wallpaper reminded him how she had liked yellow daisies. The pouring rain—it came in onslaughts again the second day—brought to mind long, open-mouthed kisses while he held her thin, soapy body in the shower, before the illness took away her ability to stand.

Tom pulled the cheap motel blanket up over his head, like a child hiding from the bogeyman. Now the sound of the pouring rain mixed with the sound and scent of his own breathing.

You couldn't trick grief any more than you could outwit death, he knew. He might lie here under the slick motel coverlet forever, but the facts remained. His old life of comfort and joy was done. He did not expect ever to be happy again; he had had enough happiness to last several lifetimes. His job now and from here forward was simply to put one foot in front of the other. He must not fail to remain grateful for what he'd once had. A Cornish poet put it aptly:

> They shall grow not old, as we that are left grow old:
> Age shall not weary them, nor the years condemn.
> At the going down of the sun and in the morning,
> We will remember them.

Tom's cell phone rang and at the far end chirped the relentlessly cheery voice of the woman who believed she was his sister. "I'm here in the lobby," Michelle said. She sounded excited. Then again, she nearly always sounded excited. About everything. "Are you ready to see Mom's house?"

Mom's house. His own mum was alive, of course, still living in her cozy cottage in Cornwall, chatting it up with her friends, and doing her best to keep Tom from what she called "his heavy brooding." *She* hadn't brooded when his da had died—but then, there was no escaping the fact that his father's death had come as something of a relief to them all.

~

The house on Ararat Street, the catch-pit of his inheritance, delivered a bit of a shock in the flesh. It was far smaller than he'd imagined. It was a tiny box of a thing. Perhaps he'd been foxed into thinking all American houses were palatial. There were television shows that featured the insides of these supersize mansions, front and back staircases, game rooms the size of airplane hangars, channels dedicated to their upkeep and repair. His mum was addicted to watching these shows.

This was a modest cottage on a busy street that, had it been transplanted someplace quiet and out of the way, would have fit well in his corner of Falmouth—not the posh upscale part of it, either. His mum would have called it "a hobbit house." But Tom instinctively approved of any human being who could keep her ecological footprint this small. It was the first hint he'd had of some affinity to the woman who had passed away.

Michelle fit her key into the lock and fumbled at its turning, pushing the door open, pausing to furtively wipe her eyes on her sleeve—Tom looked away, not to intrude on her emotion. The air smelled to him musty and acrid, like something locked up too long inside a box, but Michelle breathed in deeply. The smile she beamed on him was genuine.

"Welcome," she said, gesturing around—he wasn't sure at what. To him the house smelled of recent sickness. It was uncomfortably crowded with objects and that made the small space feel even more claustrophobic. The heavy window curtains were drawn tight; indoors, it was more like dusk than day.

"Lovely," he said, "innit."

Michelle came a few steps farther inside and touched a china figurine, then the fringed beading of a table lamp. She switched on the light rather than opening the curtains. "Hard to imagine five of us crammed in here, but we loved it. Louisa slept in the attic."

"Were there five?" said Tom, doing the counting in his head. Was there yet another sibling still to meet? His heart sank at the thought.

"My Swedish grandfather lived with us," she said. "When we were small. I could barely understand a word he said. —You have a very interesting accent, yourself."

"Do I, yeah?" said Tom. He'd never thought about it.

"You don't sound like the British actors on TV," she said. "I suppose most of them must live in London."

"I think most live in Hollywood by now," he said drily.

She poked one shoe toe into the carpet, making patterns. "Does anyone ever call you Michael?" she asked. By Michelle's gesture, and the fact that she didn't look up at him, he understood that the question might be more important that it seemed. "I just wondered."

As she spoke she removed her coat and gestured for his jacket. She hung them both on short wooden pegs. His eyes began to adjust to the gloom. Everything *looked* neat enough, and yet there were crumbs on the carpet, and half-filled water glasses in the living room. Piles of newspapers. It felt as if someone were hiding there, still.

Objects were arranged tightly in clusters of five and seven and eight. Most people arranged things in threes. The recent track of a wheeled bed had left its grooves in the pale carpet. A magnifying glass lay atop of a stack of dusty magazines. "My mum uses one of those," he said without thinking.

"Your—oh, of course," Michelle said. "Your mother is still alive?"

"Yes," he said. "And to answer your question, no one calls me Michael—but some folks claim that Saint Michael is the patron saint of Cornwall."

"Really?" She rewarded him with a watery smile. "Is that right? Saint Michael?"

"However," Tom admitted, "Saint Piran gets all the local publicity. His first disciples were a badger, a fox, and a bear. Still, Saint Michael's the more exciting saint, innit?"

"Is he?" Michelle said. She began tidying up, carrying things away into another room, presumably into a kitchen as tiny as this room. Tom just stood there, not wanting to step any farther. He fought to get his bearings. Something about the house kept him uneasy. It was dark as a shaft with the drapes and blinds drawn.

"Saint Michael led the fight against Satan and all," he called after her. "He was an archangel. Big-time stuff."

"Yes I guess he was, wasn't he?" Michelle came back into the room carrying an armful of folded dish towels. "You'll have to excuse me. I'm not very religious. And my husband is Jewish."

"Oh, I don't believe in God," said Tom. "If I did, I'd have to say he was a nasty bugger."

Michelle laughed, a short bark of surprise. Her eyes lit up when she laughed. "Well, don't let Joe hear you say it. He'll argue religion with you all day long. And Sierra—well, she's at that age where she questions everything. And I do mean, everything!"

"I'm still at that age," admitted Tom. "Couple more blackberry seasons."

"Probably a good thing—don't you think?" Her voice was light, but her expression looked anxious. She often stood with her hands curled into fists. This was a woman, Tom realized, who never stopped worrying about her child for a single solitary moment. No wonder she had circles under her eyes. The eyes were as blue as field speedwell. "That is a good sign, isn't it, that Sierra questions everything?"

"Hard to say." He instantly regretted his words. The worry fell like a hammer on her. He should have lied. Michelle had that kind of pale complexion that showed every flicker of emotion. Like the sky over Saint Ives, shifting instant by instant.

"I suppose we should—get on." He gestured toward the rest of the house.

She blushed. "Of course." She set the folded dish towels down on a sagging old chair that still carried a faint imprint of its owner. He could picture the old woman sitting there, in the same spot, day after day. "Well, this is the living room, of course. Mother collected figurines . . ." Michelle walked to a glass-fronted cabinet filled with ugly gnomish figures.

"Yeah," he said, barely glancing at it. Good Lord! Was he supposed to admire these daft objects? Surely she didn't expect him to cart them back to England?

But Michelle led him out of the living room into a tiny galley kitchen that might have fit onto the back of a houseboat. "And this is the kitchen," she said.

He nodded. Again, he was struck by the sheer number of individual objects in the room. At least sunlight poured in through the back door. There were knickknacks on every horizontal surface. Islands of salt and pepper shakers sat huddled together, as if held by elastic bands. If you thought you were going to run out of things, that you had this one last chance on earth to acquire objects, this was the place to come. Tom's own seaside cottage in Cornwall was monastic by comparison. One pot, one kettle, two plates, bowls, and cups. He and Claudia had lived a simple, stripped-down, cloistered existence—a world to themselves. He recalled reading that Thoreau kept only three chairs in his cabin on Walden Pond: "One for solitude, two for friendship, three for society." One chair too many, in Tom's opinion.

"Mom hardly cooked for herself anymore," Michelle mused, leaning against a kitchen counter, her arms folded tightly across her stomach. Her forehead was still puckered, her thoughts likely far away. He should have said something reassuring about her girl Sierra, about teenagers in general. Not that he knew much about young people—or about anything else, for that matter.

How many salt shakers did one person need? Tom had counted a dozen sets already. Wonky cream pitchers sat huddled together at one end of the table like passengers on a crowded ship.

"But Mom made wonderful meals when we were young. On Saturday nights, she'd make a crown roast, and Sunday she'd put the leftovers through a metal grinder and make roast beef hash. Oh, I wonder whatever happened to that wonderful grinder . . ."

"If we can find it, you're welcome to it," said Tom.

She flinched as if he'd slapped her.

"Michelle," he said, as gently as he could. Another woman's name felt strange in his mouth. He rummaged around for the right words, the right degree of kindness. At the same time his brain was automatically collecting and storing information about the kitchen; the deeply worn, uneven path on the linoleum floor. He could picture the old woman making her crooked way, up and down and across these same rooms—hauling . . . what? The image that came to mind was of ants, bearing heavy loads of crumbs.

"Your mum meant well, naming me in her will as she did. It was kind. I didn't come here to nip things. I just don't need—things," he finished lamely.

"Why *did* you come, then?" she asked. There were those clear blue wildflower eyes. Wide open. He'd seen them in the mirror, questioning himself in just this way. They both had children's eyes, compared to most.

"I don't know," he said. "I'm muddled by it myself." She still looked confused. He flapped one hand at her. "You have enough worries. I'm just here to help, yeah? That's all. Let's go up, have a look?"

He looked out at the hall, and something made him stop. His breath came short. What was there to be afraid of? His tracker's instinct warned him to go on up ahead—but how could he preempt this woman's right to lead? He was the stranger here. No question about that. Michelle picked up an empty teacup from the counter, looked inside it like someone reading tea leaves, then sighed and put it back down again and led the way up the steep, narrow stairs.

He breathed an audible sigh of relief when she opened the door to reveal the mother's little bedroom. She snapped on an overhead light. For once his instincts had gone awry. Nothing fearful here. It looked like any other old woman's bedroom—white coverlet over the single bed, with its tufts of pastel embroidered flowers, the head of the bed cluttered with small decorative pillows. Above, framed prints of birds. Dust, of course, in all the hard-to-reach places, and things left to lie where an elderly person's poor eyesight no longer noticed—a paper handkerchief dropped like an autumn leaf beneath a bureau; a white pain-relief tablet that had rolled into a corner. There were books on the bedside table, chiefly novels, and one book on bird-watching.

"She was a great reader," said Michelle, following his gaze.

"So am I," he said. Again, he noticed the curious pattern of wear on the floor, almost a groove in the soft pine wood, and the image again came of ants moving back and forth along a preordained path. Ants carry one hundred times their own body weight, could shift the pads on their feet, and do it all hanging upside down if need be. The tracks here led elsewhere. "So there's just this one bedroom, then?"

She shook her head. "There's a bedroom in the attic. And the little guest room down the hall. But my mom never used the others, once we kids moved out."

His heart sank. "Didna?" he said, reverting into Cornish dialect, as he always did when ill at ease. He moved instinctively toward the bedroom door, to block her way.

"Well, she never had any guests. Not overnight, I mean." Michelle stopped and cocked her head at him in the doorway. She was wearing a bright-red cotton vest, and it made her look like a robin. She hopped forward a few steps, toward him. She stopped. "What's wrong?" she asked.

"Nothing," he said.

Her forehead wrinkled a little. Did she think he suspected her of hiding valuables away? Again, out of nowhere he felt the sudden onrush of despair, like a foul wind: the impossibility of ever again being truly known.

"Didn't you want to see the other rooms?" she asked.

"Not really," Tom said. "Would you like some luncheon? You must be empty as a keg."

"We just had breakfast." She smiled at him indulgently, as if he were a willful child. "Let's take a quick look."

You'd have thought he smelled a tiger's scat somewhere. The danger seemed to be coming from right overhead. He was surprised she didn't look up at the ceiling herself, alarmed. All of his hard-won instincts warned him against going further. Giss on, he told himself.

As they stepped out of the bedroom, his eye went straight to the back of the hallway, the darkness that led to a second set of stairs. A nearly visible path was worn down that hall, ground into the flat carpet. Michelle stopped before they reached the end. He felt the hairs on the back of his neck prickle as they walked toward it. Secrets. But she was opening the guest room door, and it, too, revealed nothing fearful. Two single beds, draped in girlish quilts, school pennants hanging on the walls. Sunlight streamed in through the uncurtained window. Compared to the rest of the house, this room was almost bare. Yet this didn't make him feel any easier.

"Well done then," he said.

She nodded. He nearly had her. She half turned to go. Then she narrowed her eyes, remembering. He'd overstepped himself, and reminded her of a place she might otherwise have forgotten.

"We really should check out the attic, too," she said.

"No need," he said desperately.

"Don't be silly." She smiled. "It's no trouble at all."

Now he did keep himself in the lead. Did he think there was a madwoman hidden overhead? He smiled grimly to himself. He forced himself to walk quickly down the narrow hall. As he'd feared, the handle of the small door leading to the final set of stairs stuck a little, as if someone had been carefully closing and locking it shut, month after month, year after year.

"We might wait and come back another time," Tom said. "No rush." Once long ago he had tracked a bloody hare to its metal-toothed trap, where it lay still flopping, the life dying out of its eyes.

The wooden stairs creaked heavily under his feet, as if from too many years of bearing weight. The ceiling sloped toward his head, and he was not a tall man. Wave after wave of warning hit him. He stopped on the middle of the staircase, blocking the woman's path.

"You scared?" Michelle said teasingly, touching his shoulder. When he turned his head she was smiling as if at a balky child. He could see just the type of schoolteacher she must be. She and Claudia would have got on like toads. Michelle's students must surely love her, they would cluster around her for protection against a bitter world.

Tom's own protective instinct kept him blocking her way forward. At the least, he would not let her be the first to step inside. The boards creaked again, as if a heavy object or objects lay nearby. He felt as he would have felt approaching a dead body. His grandfather too had suffered from second sight. "It's a curse, not a gift," the old man used to tell him.

"Louisa slept up here as a teenager," Michelle said, as if to encourage him. "She liked being up on her own floor."

"Hang on," he said stepping in front of her, and ducking into the attic space.

The wreckage was bad enough to make him catch his breath. He felt rather than heard Michelle cry out with surprise as she followed close behind They could not even really both properly fit inside the attic. The small space was packed almost to the brim with things, an indoor garbage dump gone mad. It boiled and bubbled over with smashed and broken objects, with furnishings, papers, boxes, trash bags spilling over like foaming seas. If a human being had packed all of the random objects of their life into a closet every day, and kept on adding to the pile, cramming more objects, broken and whole, beneath and around the dusty mountains of accumulated junk, they might then at last have arrived at this—a cross between a doong cart and a temple holy to discarded household items.

Some of the piles reached all the way to the low attic beams. Much of it was simply trash. Tom's gaze swept across to hillocks of yellowed newspapers and tattered magazines; towers of greeting cards; piles of dirty dishes, cans, Kleenex, boxes, packed greengrocer's bags. There must have once been a bed in the room, for some of the articles were heaped horizontally as if they had been levitated: cascading heaps of paperback books; the broken household gods of statuettes and candlesticks, empty meal boxes, tins of tomatoes, rolls of paper and assorted stationer's objects: notebooks, fat logs of many yellow pencils jumbled together with twine . . .

"I need to sit down," said Michelle behind him in a faint voice. Clearly there was no room for sitting in this place, barely enough room to stand upright inside the space. It was hard to breathe. He nudged her back and down the stairs, leading her by the arm, till he had her safely back down on the second floor. There Michelle sank onto her heels in the hallway, shaking her head, steadying one hand on the wall. She kept staring at the floor in front of her, as if afraid to look up.

"I simply don't understand this," she said. "How is this possible? My mom was a very tidy person. She was a totally *normal* person. I swear." Then she covered her mouth and started laughing, rocking back and forth, finally sitting down and folding her arms across her stomach. "Wow!" she said. "Holy cow!"

"People do this kind of thing often," lied Tom.

Michelle turned her head to look at him, but it was a blind look. She covered her mouth again with her hand, still laughing. "I'm sorry," she gasped. "Not funny!"

The attic had reminded him in some ways of a snowstorm—the way that snow swirls things into fantastical shapes and towers and Gothic turrets. Some of the tilting, jagged piles of junk defied any sense of gravity. In a way, it was admirable. It hadn't happened in a day, or even a year. The chaos was immense. It was ingenious. This woman had to have been some kind of engineer to have managed it at all.

"It's called a catch-pit, back home," Tom said.

"You've seen rooms like that before, back home?" Michelle asked in a faint voice.

"Yeah sure," he lied. In truth he'd seen anything like it only once. An old widow woman in his neighborhood had died, leaving behind a cottage filled entirely with old articles of clothing, most of it little more than mildewed rags. Yet she'd gone about the village day after day, as neat as any other Cornishwoman. Her vegetable gardens had been tidy models of production and order. She was a brilliant needlewoman. You could not explain the complex madness of the human brain.

"I don't know what to say," Michelle said. Her laughter had slowly dissolved into tears, as Tom knew it would. He raised his hands helplessly.

Michelle tried to wipe her tears away with her hands. "Oh dear," she said. "My poor mother."

An old nursery rhyme popped into Tom's head unbidden, from his childhood.

> Monday for danger,
> Tuesday kiss a stranger,
> Wednesday for a letter,
> Thursday for something better,
> Friday for . . .

He couldn't remember the rest, but it ended with something about true love. His nursery teacher had led in the recitation of this and similar ditties. Here it was, a Tuesday. He leaned down and kissed this strange woman on the top of her head, as if she had really been his sister. She looked up gratefully.

"Thank you," she sniffled. "I'll be fine in a minute. I'm sorry. It's just been such a shock." She gestured helplessly. "The mess . . . All of it."

Tom supposed that he himself, a come-by-chance child dropped out of nowhere, was a part of the mess. He had grown up knowing of his strange origins. This woman had known about none of it. The shock must be immense. Yet she had been unfailingly hospitable and kind. He let her collect herself. His own mind was a naturally ordered place. Now that he had seen the worst, the attic didn't even really faze him. Another problem to be solved. Of course, she hadn't been *his* mum.

His grandfather had once suggested that Tom think of each obstacle not as a problem but as a project. A challenge. He could put it all to rights in a few days. This sort of work suited him. There was nothing to wail about, certainly. In all the time he had known and loved Claudia, she had never shed a tear in front of him. Not at the first diagnosis of MS. Not later, when her body betrayed her, shifting the terms of the disease each time. For one full week she'd lost her sight entirely. Another time it was her sense of smell. Everything, she'd confessed to him laughing, smelled like carpet cleaner. Never once had he caught her weeping. Not even at the bitter end, when she'd had every possible reason to carry on.

The truth was, crying women irritated him. He had always had to struggle against his own disgust, an impulse to bolt.

"Chin up," he said. "Could be worse. No corpses up there at any rate, no chopped-up body parts."

Michelle forced out a laugh with a sob mixed in it. She wiped away tears with the fingers of both hands, smudging her makeup.

"I'll bide till we get it sorted," he said, if only because her tears were annoying him and he didn't know what he was saying. He had to say something to get her to stop her crying. "People have their reasons. They always have their reasons. We'll get it sorted out. It's all right, innit?" He lapsed back into Cornish at moments like these.

"You're being so incredibly kind," she said. She peered down the dark hall again. "Oh my God," she added. "—I forgot about Louisa. We've got to get some of that mess cleared out before Louisa lays eyes on it. We have to. It would be the absolute last straw."

Tom suspected that he had been the second-to-last straw. "Course we will," he said soothingly. "We'll get hold of a few skips—dumpsters—and before you know it this small house'll be empty as a keg."

She was sitting on the floor now, her chin resting on her knees, peering up at him, still sniffling. Her trousers must be getting all dusty. "Oh, a dumpster!" she said, lighting up. The strangest things made these people happy—or sad. "That's a marvelous idea."

"Easy." He put out one hand and hauled her to her feet. Ah, he was a dirty liar. It would all be anything but easy. He'd have to change his plane ticket, let his mum and his clients know. Who could predict how much this latest bit would delay his returning home? No good deed ever went unpunished. And what would make an old woman keep hold of every scrap she'd ever laid hands on? She must have lost a good deal.

"We'll buy a box of those city garbage bags," said Michelle. "A case, even. We'll rent a dumpster. And you'll stay a little longer? Really? Your boss wouldn't mind?" There were tears clinging to her eyelashes, like dew on the furze. The things up in the attic seemed to be leaning down toward him, as if waiting for his reply. He thought with longing of his little cot, his empty stretch of rocky shingle with nothing but the blowing sea wind fluting in long undulations across it.

"I'm my own boss," he said. He hoped it didn't sound as if he were bragging. The opposite, more like. He was a freelance consultant, a hired gun, jack-of-all-trades.

"And you'll move out of that dreary motel, won't you?" the woman said. Oh, she was a sly one. Crafty, was what she was. "There's so much extra room at our house! We have three guest rooms. Sierra's taken a shine to you somehow. She doesn't like many people. You'll stay with us."

"That I won't," he said. "I'll stay right here in this house till the job is done." He trod one foot on the worn floorboards, to make it clear. She rewarded him with a watery smile, as brilliant as a Cornish rainbow.

She's caught you hook, line, and sinker, said Claudia, but she sounded pleased as punch.

CHAPTER EIGHT

By the time the other sister, Louisa, came by to view the attic, Tom had gotten much of the obvious rubbish cleared and carted out of the way. Out of sight, out of mind. Most of it was simply trash, and he didn't have to think about tossing it. He filled nine or ten large trash sacks with old yellowing newspapers. These went to a recycling center. There was a certain satisfaction to sifting through so much mess; a microversion of what he did for a living, he supposed, sorting through records: checking facts and backgrounds, skimming through court proceedings and unearthing hidden bank accounts. He liked seeking out the shreds of order hidden inside of chaos.

Michelle had called her husband Joe, who seemed to know every man, woman, and child in every corner of the city of Worcester. Joe was a useful person, seemingly unflappable. By five that first afternoon a twenty-yard dumpster had pulled into the old woman's driveway. Tom used the clean-up job as an excuse to send the chatty younger sister away—"I can't do my work with someone looking on, cannit?" and figured out a simple, methodical sorting system. He had to work fast or he'd never be done.

He made five piles: one of errant and absolute rubbish; one to recycle (torn envelopes, old newspapers, magazines and circulars; broken plastic objects, empty cans of fizzy drinks and so on); one that might be given away to charity; one pile of potentially valuable objects; and one very small pile for himself. This last, of course, was only at Michelle's stubborn insistence. There was nothing in the attic room—or in any room in the crowded little house, come to that—of remotest interest to Tom. He thought instead of his mum, and his few mates back home who might like some sort of souvenir of his strange American adventure. One man he knew collected carved wooden ducks. All right. As long as the duck was not a precious or well-made object—Tom was determined to carry away nothing of any real financial value—he could take it home. There were two such ducks buried under a mound of clutter on the windowsill. One was signed, with lifelike eyes. The other was clumsier, the body more squat. Tom took the unsigned piece and set it aside.

Even though he'd made a decent dent in the mess, the sister Louisa seemed initially gobsmacked by the ruinous attic. Her jaw hung open. Tom remembered now that this had once been Louisa's bedroom, after the death of the Swedish grandfather. That would make it even worse for her.

Michelle had done her best to prepare her sister for what lay inside the attic room on Ararat. Louisa's own room! More secrets, more bad news. It was a conversation Michelle found that she both dreaded and relished—which she believed was not unusual among family members. You hated breaking the awful news, and at the same time you could hardly wait to tell the only other person in the world to whom it could ever really matter. Michelle had phoned her sister in the late afternoon—after Louisa's daily after-work glass of wine, but before supper, she hoped—and asked Louisa when was the last time she'd gone all the way upstairs and looked around their mother's house.

"I went all the time," said Louisa, bristling. "Why do you ask?"

"All the time—really?"

"Why?" insisted Louisa. "Don't tell me you found another brother hidden up there."

Michelle forced a smile. Then she realized Louisa couldn't see whether she was smiling or frowning over the phone. "I mean, even the attic?"

There was a silence at the other end. "Why would I go into the attic?" asked Louisa. "There was nothing left up there. —Was there?"

"Well, yes, there were some things," said Michelle.

"Please tell me it's a pile of gold, and not another long-lost relative," said Louisa.

"Ha ha. No. It's just—some—items," said Michelle.

"What kind of items?" Louisa asked. "Anything worth anything? I hope?"

"No. I just think you might want to see it for yourself," said Michelle. "Don't freak out, please. It's no big deal. Just stay calm—"

"I'm coming straight there," said Louisa, and hung up.

So there they were together, that same afternoon up in the airless attic, the two sisters staring around as if they'd landed on another planet.

"I just don't believe it," muttered Louisa. "Jesus H."

"I didn't believe it either," answered Michelle. "Not at first."

"Maybe some stranger snuck in and filled it with crap." To Tom's relief, Louisa didn't look his way when she said this.

"Mom was full of surprises," said Michelle, which set them both off into gales of laughter. Seemed like these Americans were always either crying or laughing.

"Yeah, well, she sure as hell surprised us enough," said Louisa, but she didn't look as cuffed as usual. She wasn't frowning, her face didn't have its usual taut, severe expression. Bemused, more like. Almost filled with wonder. She reached out one finger and tapped the chipped handle of a broken cup.

"Tell me," she said, "why anyone on earth would keep this."

"Just in case?" said Michelle. She was bent over some low bookshelves, reading book titles.

"In case of what?"

Michelle shrugged. She looked at the broken cup.

"Tell me what would make this object useful," said Louisa. "The apocalypse?" But her tone was more teasing than mad.

It was like a scene from a children's fairy tale. An enchanted castle turned to sludge. The two sisters slowly made their way around the attic shoulder to shoulder, mouths open. Now and again they would stop, point at some random object. It made Tom feel as if he were intruding on an intimate moment, something he was never intended to be part of.

Tom kept out of their way, melting back into a corner without a sound. He had long ago learned how to make himself invisible; though he was not nearly as adept at it as his granddad, it was a skill that came in handy. He'd let the sisters sort things out for themselves. It had been their mother, after all. He went and hid for a while in their morsel of a backyard, till it seemed safe to reappear.

This latest discovery of the wreck in the attic, instead of throwing Louisa into a deeper funk, as she might have expected, came as almost a comfort. It felt as if she'd discovered that her mother had a secret depth, a gift for painting, or some other hidden quality. And it made Louisa feel remarkably lucky. The only thing she ever collected was paper bags, for recycling. She'd grown so used to thinking of everything about herself as not exactly right, maybe even downright bad—a *wicked pissah*, as folks in Wormtown would say. Now in comparison to her own mom, Louisa felt not wicked at all, but surprisingly normal. She looked in the mirror and didn't hate the amused face she saw there.

She wore her hair pulled tightly back in a bright-yellow hairband. Once in a while she just had to have some dab of color somewhere. Art hated anything showy, anything that stood out too much, but still. She tried to take in the enormity of the mess around her. Wait till Art gets a load of this, Louisa thought, snorting.

She picked her way slowly through the towers in the attic, holding her breath in the hot, dry air, she and Michelle studying the piles of things like visitors going through a museum in another country.

Her poor mother had saved—well, apparently, she had tried to save everything.

She appeared never to have thrown anything away, no matter how pathetic or used or broken. Old makeup cases, scented candles, bottles of shampoo. Balls of pastel yarn, plastic bags bristling with knitting needles—Louisa had never once seen her mother knit—piles of skimpy hand towels, most of them seasonal: decorated with bunnies, pumpkins, embroidered Christmas trees. A vast number of small stuffed animals. Little boxes cached inside of more boxes. One wrong move could send the whole attic, maybe the whole house toppling down. It made every mess Louisa had ever made in her whole messy life seem like nothing. And this, Michelle informed her, was after they'd already gone and cleared out the worst of it.

Michelle was chewing on her cuticles, a nervous habit she'd had as a child. Louisa batted at her hand to make her stop.

"I wonder if it bothered Mom, keeping all this hidden from us," said Michelle. "It would have bothered me. It would *haunt* me, knowing I had this much stuff packed away in my house."

"Well, Mom kept some secrets," Louisa said. "Makes you wonder what else we didn't know."

"Maybe she was a bank robber," offered Michelle wanly.

"Maybe she was a ninja."

"Maybe she worked for the FBI. Or the CIA!" suggested Michelle.

"Maybe she was an astronaut," laughed Louisa. "A race-car driver. A Russian spy."

"Maybe she was bonkers," said Michelle, sobering up. Louisa stopped laughing too.

Both sisters mused on that in silence for a moment.

"More likely she threw spare clothes in here for storage, and the next thing you know, it turns into—" Tom lifted his arm to indicate.

The two sisters examined him with identical expressions. It was clear that they'd forgotten he was in the house. Tom made himself recede from view again, and they went on talking around him.

"Do you think maybe she really was crazy?" Michelle asked Louisa, her brow furrowing. "I mean, do you think she might have been mentally ill? Her mom did commit suicide, you know. So there's that."

"Mom was perfectly sane," said Louisa. Louisa was the expert. She had the degree in psychology and social work. Her word, at least in these matters, was law. "I don't think you can call someone crazy just because they are—you know. Eccentric."

"Right," put in Tom, despite himself. He meant to keep quiet. People back at home had called Claudia eccentric too—only that wasn't the word they used. They called her barmy, and close, and deep, and addled, and other insulting words no emmet would understand. Maybe this woman, Alma, had thought she'd been rescuing these strange objects from oblivion.

Claudia had rescued every living thing in sight. Foxes and rabbits and squirrels and mice—wild things mostly. She saved wounded domestics, too, including dogs and blind cats and once a pair of goats. After Claudia died, Tom vowed never to keep another living creature in his house. It took months to release the wild ones back where they belonged, and to place every rescue with some other caretaker—the last to go was a cantankerous three-legged hare named Heller.

That was why Cain slew Abel and not the other way around, Tom thought. Because the animal lovers were mad and gentle, and the people who loved flowers and trees couldn't be trusted in the end. They'd shoot you if you stepped on their precious delphiniums. Tom knew this well enough. He often preferred plants to animals and people, himself.

Michelle shook out a rumpled bedsheet, releasing a cloud of dust into the air. All three of them went into sneezing fits at once. The oddest thing was, they all sneezed the same exact way—making a high-toned, small, sharp, clearly articulated *"A-choo!"* at the end of the sneeze. Could such a small, peculiar thing be genetic? It was the first sign that all three were actually biologically connected. Louisa looked surprised, Michelle appeared delighted, and Tom felt something close to alarm.

Like it or no, these people were his people. "Whithersoever thou goest . . ." as the Bible said. They were tangled with each other far down the blood line, bound together by people long dead and gone, glued by fine-tuned DNA enzymes, thinner than the hairs on a fiddle bow, soldering them. Claudia had felt herself connected to every living thing on the face of the earth, including lowly dung beetles and worms. Her generosity knew no bounds. But Tom was not like his great beloved. This reminder of connection made him uneasy, as if someone had stuck Sellotape all over him, had trapped and bound him somehow. It made him want to yank himself free and bolt.

His time in America was running out soon, thank God. A handful of days, and he'd have done his part. And not a moment too soon, either. Michelle was becoming attached. She had an adhesive personality, Tom thought. That was in her nature, as solitude and silence was his. She stuck to her husband like a shadow to a post; she hovered over her teenage daughter; she kept coming round and round the mother's house to stay tied to those apron strings as well. If she had been a stray dog or cat, always needing to be petted, Tom would have said she had been weaned too soon. But some people were like that, naturally; human burrs. Once, long ago, he'd had a girlfriend like that. Just one. He shook free of that as soon as possible. But you could tell Michelle's husband Joe thrived on it, both the attention and the feeling of being needed. Lots of men did.

Michelle laid claim to a slew of items up in the attic—junk you couldn't have given away in the mangiest charity shop. She filled bags and bags with this wonky stuff. Lamps and souvenirs and who-knows-what. The more sensible older sister Louisa wanted nothing but one small shoebox of keepsakes—but it was the teenager, Sierra, who kept coming back to sort and organize things, day after day.

All kinds of crazy little things delighted her. Sierra exclaimed over tiny glass bottles with cork stoppers thinner than her fingernails. She gathered up her grandmother's greeting cards, wrapping paper, bookmarks, and buttons and bore them away to do who knew what with the treasures. She was very polite, always asking Tom's permission first, unwilling to claim so much as a paperclip without his explicit say-so. Once she found a set of four hand-painted lunch plates—at least they looked hand painted. Bright colors, oddly familiar style. "Is this too much?" she asked him.

"Four small plates? Hardly. Nothing's too much," Tom said. "Just take it. Take it all."

He'd be glad if she carted the whole house away, one plate at a time if she liked. Even so, the youngster was the only one who didn't actually get on Tom's nerves. She was organized, patient, and a hard worker. It was Sierra who made them all form a human chain so they could hand things down the stairs and out the door to the skip the most efficient way possible. Sierra knew how to hold her tongue. Michelle would perch on a box in the cramped quarters of the attic and chatter till his head spun. He'd never known anyone who had so many words inside them. Louisa mostly kept to the other parts of the house, but her presence, to someone as solitary as Tom, was like the smell of burning paper. He sensed her acrid fuming even when she was on a different level of the house.

All these Americans wandered in and out of each other's space in a way he found extraordinary, and distressing. Tom longed for his solitude. He was lonely for his loneliness. He missed the wood stairs leading down to the empty strand at dawn, the roar of water scraping against sand. Neighbors didn't pay aimless calls on each other in his part of Cornwall—or anyhow he'd trained them not to pay such calls on him. But these people here were ineducable. Neighbors and friends dropped by all the time, seemingly for no reason at all. Even the mailman came inside to pay a social visit. He stood in the middle of the tiny living room twirling his blue cap in his hands. Mailbag over his shoulder. When he spoke of the late Alma Johansson there were actual tears in his eyes.

Only Sierra set to work as soon as she came into the house. She settled her school things down in a corner by the door and set to the task at hand. For a teenager, she was curiously focused. Most young people were an aimless and sociable lot, always staring at their gadgets. And she generally kept a cool head. One evening, just toward twilight, Sierra cantered down from the attic and said, "There's something flying around up there. Maybe a bird. It's flying funny."

"What do you mean, funny?" said Michelle. She and Louisa were paging through some picture albums.

"It sailed over my head," the girl said. "Twice." She imitated the fluttering movement with her hand.

"Sounds like a bat," said Tom.

"A bat!" The two grown women shrieked the word at the same time and headed for the front door. Tom had never seen either one move that fast. Michelle called, "Come on, Sierra! Right now!"

"Most bats are harmless as mice," said Tom.

"I want to see it," said Sierra.

"Oh my God," said Louisa, half laughing, half sobbing. She was pulling at the doorknob.

"Sierra, come *on*!" shrilled her mother.

"I want to see the bat," Sierra repeated.

"You two go outside," said Tom, pushing them out of the house. They bolted out quick enough, glancing nervously over their shoulders, as if they expected the thing to come swooping after them.

Tom and Sierra headed up the stairs.

"You're not going to kill it, are you?" said Sierra. "Please don't murder it! Bats are protected. We learned about them in science class." As if they'd be any less precious if she hadn't learned about them.

"We're not killing anything," Tom said. He wished he felt half as sure as he sounded.

"Maybe we can catch it with a towel," Sierra suggested. "I heard of someone doing that."

She ran lightly ahead to fetch it. Tom wished he had his fishing hat on. The one thing he couldn't stand was the idea of a bat flying into his hair. Then he remembered he didn't have hair anymore, none left to speak of. One less thing to worry about. Sierra looked around the attic, interested, not at all panicked. Tom eased a window all the way open.

The bat was swooping through the high spaces of the room. It looked all right, not sick at any rate. There was always something unearthly about the creature's grace.

"Looks more like swimming than flying," said Sierra.

Yes, he thought. And now what? "Okay," Tom said, reaching for the towel. "I'll take these two corners, and you'll take the others, and we'll make a sort of net."

"You're sure we're not going to hurt it?" she asked.

"Dead sure," he lied. *What next?* he thought. His da could have coaxed the bat out of the room just by talking to it. Tom lacked those skills. But the longer he stewed about it, the harder it would get.

The girl moved first. She stepped in, shoulder first, as if in the opening moves of a dance, and the bat swooped, and somehow they got the towel curled around it, and the next thing Tom knew, the bat and the towel were sailing out the open window, toward the porch roof below. They watched the thing land, shake itself, moving the towel around like a miniature ghost, then break free of it altogether and flutter away.

"Imagine if it flew right at Mom and Aunt Lou," Sierra said, laughing. She sometimes covered her mouth when she laughed.

"That would go over well," agreed Tom.

He realized he had not thought of Claudia at all in the last few minutes. She would have loved the bat. *I will accept no severing of our love,* he thought, remembering some poem or other. His hands clenched into fists. He refused to forget. Not Claudia. He would keep her with him to the furthest ends of time.

Sierra stood by the open window, looking down. "I'm going to have to wash that towel," she said.

"We'd best find the crack where it came in, and seal it," said Tom.

"Good job," they said together, at the same time.

You felt like you'd won an award when you made her grin, he realized.

If Sierra had any mates at all, he never laid eyes on them, and she never mentioned any. She seldom talked about school. No one ever accompanied her. She was always alone. She never referred to her illness, either, not after that first ride from the airport, though often he could hear the faint sound of her monitor, and she always smelled to him like plastic tubing and Bactine.

Sierra, he suspected, was not what folks called "book smart." She didn't hide her disdain for school. "Borrring," she said. She was clever enough in other ways, however. Michelle needn't fret so much. Sierra possessed the mind of a natural-born engineer, a person who could do practical things. She'd sorted the house things into sensible piles, and indefatigably moved chairs and tables around from place to place, not just in the attic room, but in the rest of the house as well. Her company was restful as a cat compared to the others. She kept to her quiet corners, he kept to his.

She reminded Tom of a cautious one-eyed calico stray that Claudia had scooped up from the hands of death. The girl and the cat had both been ill, come to think of it, though the cat died when it was still barely more than a kitten. Some things could not be rescued, Tom reminded himself.

Tom had exchanged his return ticket home for an open-ended return, hoping that one more week would mark the end of it. He'd had no time for roaming the fields, no time for tracking, though the deep green New England woods extended in all directions around Ararat

Street. He'd heard there were moose and bears about, but he never caught sight of them. Not even a deer or a rabbit. He'd never lived so much indoors. Sometimes it felt as if he had moved into a cage.

He stepped from concrete to tarmac to wall-to-wall carpet, his feet barely touching grass. At home, in Cornwall, at the southern margin of the land he walked barefoot along the strand at least five kilometers a day. Yet he was not unhappy here—or rather, he was not entirely, soddenly miserable, and that in itself was a welcome change.

He postponed his few current clients, pushing them back a few weeks. No one would notice the difference, or care. The work he did left no visible trace in the universe. In the end, his clients did what they wanted to do, regardless of his faithful research. He'd once unearthed a really underhanded, dodgy scheme at a line of dry cleaners, stretching from Pembury to Bath, giving new meaning to the phrase *money laundering*. But in the end his client bought the chain of stores anyway. Made a fortune at them, too.

Tom's life had long ago narrowed to two joys, twin comforts: Claudia, and the natural world—his beloved's eyes, and the scattershot of bronze watery reflection circling out toward Saint Just. What more did any human being want or need? But there was Sierra, cooing softly over toothpick holders and bone-china soap dishes. She appeared content. It seemed too peaceful to last, and of course it was.

A day later, the girl slammed into the little house, rattling the glass in the front door. Now he'd have to repair that, too. It was just past noon. That was the first sign of something off the mark. Sierra always came close to four, after her high school let out. Reliable as rain. She crashed around downstairs, cursing. He'd never heard her use foul language before either. Tom made just enough sound that she'd know he was upstairs. With the mood she was in, he didn't want to startle her. After a decent interval he came down to the kitchen and found the girl's eyes red rimmed from crying.

It wasn't in his nature to ask a stranger what was wrong, pry into someone else's personal life. "Cuppa?" he said.

She swung around like an angry animal, eyes blazing. *"What?"*

"Cup, of, tea?" he said, as slowly as possible.

"Why don't you just talk normal English?" she said.

He shrugged, and smiled wryly.

She said, half-grudgingly, "I guess we're the ones speaking another language."

"Cream or plain?"

She made a face. "Plain I guess. Nobody my age drinks tea." But she pulled up a wobbly wooden chair to the table, and ran her fingers through her dark hair, tugging at the ends. She glowered down at the kitchen tabletop. "Dumb fudging jerks."

"Because they don't drink tea?"

"The jerks who run my fudging school," she seethed. "They think I'm stupid. I'm not stupid. I hate them all." She didn't add anything else, and he didn't ask.

Better not to get mixed up in it. She was scrumped up like a toad on a hot shovel. Even sitting there, she was irritably twitching about. One knee kept jiggling up and down. Her toes hammered against the kitchen floor. The day was hot and humid. Tom plumped the kettle, lit the hob, opened the fridge, which held no more than an apple, an orange, a pint of milk, and a container of yogurt. He felt a sudden overwhelming homesick longing for a kebab shop and the smell of the English tide.

"I could run out for something," he said. He didn't know what the girl was or wasn't allowed to eat. He knew there were strict food rules.

"I already ate," she said.

He suspected she was lying. It seemed to him perhaps the girl had lost quite a bit of weight recently. She wasn't all that big to begin with. Her trousers sagged, and she tugged her long T-shirts down almost to her knees. He didn't know if that was a good or a bad sign, either—something else to research.

He poured the tea and she did nothing but stir it in circles. She didn't take out the tea bag, but let the beverage turn amber brown, and then nearly coffee colored. Neither of them spoke. Finally the girl said shakily, "I need to call my mom."

He nodded, relieved. "Sounds like," he said, hoping to sound like a responsible adult.

She slumped into the next room, and Tom could hear the tearful murmuring of her voice talking into the phone. Then her volume rose and he caught a phrase or two. "I *did* tell them!" she shouted and then, louder, "I can handle it myself!"

Within minutes Michelle was charging into the house, calling out her daughter's name. Sierra had gone back to her endless sorting upstairs, dragging things around. It must have calmed her in some way. After a while he'd heard her humming under her breath, and the tinny sound of some popular song escaping through headphones. Michelle came charging into the kitchen, wild eyed. "Did you hear what happened?" she asked him.

"Trouble?" he said. He hoped she wouldn't tell him.

"They're making Sierra change schools," she said. "The bastards." Something thumped upstairs, then scraped. "How long has she been here?" Michelle asked.

He never wore a watch. At home, he never needed one. "Dunno. An hour," he guessed.

"It's all about protecting their goddamn state test scores," Michelle fumed. All her golden sunniness had darkened. "No wonder she hates it there. They called her into guidance, Sierra along with two others, and gave them their marching orders. Kicked the kids out. Trying to move them to a dumb-ass special academy, pardon my French."

"Hm." Academy. He pictured a place full of ancient statuary and trees. Didn't sound too terrible to him.

"It's a parking lot for the underachievers," she said, reading his expression. "It's a dumping ground. Gets them out of the way. Most of the schoolwork is done online, sitting in front of a computer. You might as well drop your kid at the post office and let them sit there all day like an unclaimed package. Honey!" she called suddenly, her tone shifting entirely. "Can you please come down here so I can see your pretty face?"

"No!" Sierra roared back.

"Have you eaten?" Michelle called.

"Yes!" answered the roar.

Michelle shook her head. She chewed nervously at the side of her finger. "I don't know," she said, flexing and straightening her hands. She tossed her head so her golden hair flew in front of her face. "I hate this. I guess maybe she'll adjust to a new place," she said. "I don't know. I'm a teacher, so I *should* know, but it's different when it's your own child. You feel so helpless."

He sipped his tea, keeping his eyes fixed on the rim of the cup. He understood about helpless, even if he knew nothing about raising children.

"I guess it'll be okay," Michelle added. "Maybe it'll be fine. She hasn't been thriving where she is. At least she's not the only student being booted out."

They sat silent a moment, listening to the scraping and banging sounds from upstairs. "She'll hate it," said Michelle. "I know she'll hate it. But even so—"

The tea was bitter, and growing cool. "Refuse the move," he said. "If she doesn't want it."

Her head jerked up. He held her gaze.

"What?" she said. "I don't think we have a choice."

"Yeah you do," he said. "You always have a choice. Ask your husband. He's a lawyer, innit?"

"Well, yes . . ."

"They'll be terrified of lawyers. Most wankers are."

When she smiled, Michelle suddenly looked twenty years younger. Her blue eyes shone at him. She was the pretty one in the family, no question. Then the worry came down again, the way rain settled in the cracks of rills and gorse, sending a whole field into damp chill. "Sierra's not taking her breakfast bolus," she said in a worried voice, poking at an invisible something on the tabletop. She glanced up at the ceiling. "I keep checking up on her. I may have to install a monitor alarm soon—and then she'll think I don't trust her to regulate her own diabetes meds."

"You don't," he said.

There was that cornflower-blue gaze again, fastening on his. He felt it like little hooks, tethering him to the planet. Two small frown lines above her brows, like the delicate parallel tracks of a vole. "That's awful. —It's true. I must be a terrible mother. I don't even trust my own child," she said.

"Nor should you," he added. "You can't take this stuff lightly. It's dead serious, isn't it?"

"Oh yes," she said. "It's always dead serious. Tom, you know, you could—"

"I won't be staying long," Tom interrupted her. "Don't get too attached—right? Don't let *her* get too attached to me either." He jerked his head in the direction of the girl upstairs.

Michelle smiled wryly, leaning back in her chair. She folded her arms tightly over her chest. "That's okay," she said, with an uncharacteristic bitterness in her voice. "We're used to losing family members."

CHAPTER NINE

Louisa had done a good deal of thinking since her mother passed. Died, she corrected herself. Since her mother had *died*. People in Wormtown, down-and-out knuckleheads; working-class types who drank beer from the can and spat in the street, who poked fun at themselves and laughed you to scorn if you talked about your feelings—those same tough-as-nails hard-asses called it "passing" when someone died. Showed up at your house with tears in their eyes and a big box of drugstore candy in hand.

Louisa knew that her sister Michelle kept taking it personally that Alma Johansson had died without telling her girls half of what she knew about her own life. As if Michelle were to blame for her mother's secrecy. If only she'd somehow been a better daughter, if she'd just been paying more attention, if they'd all spent more time together . . . If Sierra hadn't been so sick, if Michelle didn't let Joe take care of everything. Oh, Louisa could read her kid sister like a book. She'd always been one for taking on the burdens of the world.

But Michelle couldn't have changed her mother's basic nature. The child of a suicide no one ever talked about—it was a miracle Alma had been as happy and well adjusted as she was. Louisa knew something about hanging on to secrets. She had been keeping them all her life, for herself and for other people, too. And what did it lead to in the end? An attic space loaded full of rubbish, crammed in behind a locked door. Well, Louisa wasn't going to wait around for that to happen to her. She would give things in her own life until the end of the week, and then something had to give. When she thought of it, as sudden as that, it made her suck in her breath. You went along and played along. Still, there was a limit to everything, and in the wake of her mother's death and resurrection as a stranger Louisa had never fully known—in the wake of all that, Louisa gave herself a deadline. She had to keep it short, or she'd chicken out. Seven more days. To figure things out, get her own life in order. One week, seven days. The very idea made her breathless. She counted them off, one by one, as scared as she had ever been in her life.

Those seven days of waiting felt to Louisa like seven months. Or else like seven minutes. They went too slow, then they went too fast. Sometimes she almost gave up, gave back in. Why not? Maybe she could just let well enough alone. Her heart pounded like a wild bird at the cage of her ribs. She could feel herself shrinking backward in the middle of her workday, resisting a change even as part of her was moving inexorably forward.

She became diligent and extra careful at work and at home, as if her own forced goodness could forestall the inevitable. She cooked enough on Sunday night to feed them all week; she never once complained; she didn't pick any fights with Art; she kept the house clean. She bit her tongue and kept her smart-ass nasty remarks to herself. She even considered praying but that seemed a bit much. Hey God, remember me? Sorry about that thirty-year break I've been on. She took every needy client that called for an appointment, staying on extra late at the office till seven, eight at night, which made snooty Brandi, the WAUSA manager, raise her sculpted blonde eyebrows in surprise.

Louisa could practically feel Brandi thinking. Why is that Louisa Wandowski being so cooperative all of a sudden? She must need the overtime money pretty bad. I'll bet she screwed up royally somewhere. She must be in big trouble to be suddenly acting so nice.

I'm just avoiding going home, Louisa could have told her. I bet we've all done that sometime. But there was no talking to someone like Brandi. You might as well march yourself up to a store mannequin and give it a go. Lips outlined in mulberry, peach blush creating high round cheekbones above her real cheekbones, Brandi looked like she should have been working behind an Estée Lauder counter in some fancy Boston department store. She acted like she'd been born with a silver spoon glued to the roof of her mouth, but Louisa knew she'd grown up on the most desperate, dangerous part of Dorchester Street. That *i* at the end of her name was another dead giveaway. White trash always named their kids things like Bambi and Toni. Seemed like everyone Louisa knew was hiding some secret or other.

Louisa went into Art's little study while he was away at work, and opened his desk drawer, and rummaged around for a few minutes, found what she was looking for and then closed it again. He never bothered to lock anything because Art knew Louisa was not the kind of wife who pried.

On Monday she worked late. She went to Trivia with the gang on Wednesday night and they came in second because none of them could identify that year's Academy Award winners. No one had time to go to the movies anymore. Louisa was the history buff, so she was usually good for history and geography questions. But her mind wasn't on it; and when the MC asked a question about the Sun King, her mind drew a big fat blank.

Thursday night she and Jean-Marie went shopping together because Jean-Marie's eldest girl was getting married that summer, and Jean-Marie needed a nice mother-of-the-bride dress. The color scheme was maroon and gold; everyone in the bridal party was going to look like they were part of a marching band. Jean-Marie and Louisa drove an hour away to the big fancy Natick Mall, which was like visiting another country, filled with only rich and young people. After they found the gold-colored dress Jean-Marie had been looking for, they went and had cocktails in one of the mall chain restaurants, giggling like teenagers. Louisa and Jean-Marie had been friends since high school. They'd both lost people in that big fire up on Indigo Hill. Maybe their only true loves. It had happened so early. They never talked about it anymore, they hadn't either of them talked about it in decades, but both of them thought about it plenty.

Before she went out, Louisa cleaned her whole house from top to bottom Thursday after work, mopping and then scrubbing down on her knees, and Friday she got the car washed on her way home from work, picked up some fried chicken, but by the time she came home that night, Art was already out for the count, sprawled on his back in the spare-room bed, snoring lightly, with the door closed. He said he knew his snoring kept her awake. Not that she'd ever really cared or complained.

On Saturday morning, (Only one more day left, she told herself, just one) Louisa ate at Lou Roc's Diner with the Gang of Six. There were seven that day, including Paco's wife Kim, and an old high school friend named Scotch, who'd been away in rehab, and who sat at breakfast gulping down black coffee like it was going out of style. Art didn't come. He had too many pressing things to do around the house, he told her, and Louisa was way past arguing with him. She was running out of time now for real. The week had flown by. It was like it had never happened.

Sunday was the next day of the week, as sudden as that. She wished the Saturday-morning breakfast out with her gang at Lou Roc's could last all day. The clock on the restaurant wall seemed to be moving too fast. Maybe this was how it felt if you were a doomed inmate on death row. Maybe it was how you felt when you were nine months pregnant. Louisa didn't know—she'd never been either condemned or pregnant.

She'd lived a pretty uneventful life, all things considered. Less interesting than her own mother. She looked around at the other customers, and the waitresses jogging from table to table. It was pretty sad that she felt more at home in a Worcester diner than she did in her own living room, but that's the way it was. She looked and looked her fill at Flick Bergstrom, sitting across from her in the booth till even Jean-Marie said, "Jeez, Louise. Paint a picture, it'll last longer."

And then Louisa opened her eyes on Sunday, waking up alone in her bed, and the day was cool, for June, and overcast, and gray light filled the bedroom. Channel 5's meteorologist Harvey Leonard was predicting thunderstorms for later, and then hot weather moving in. She trusted Harvey Leonard.

Art had woken and started his day before her, as usual, and she heard the roar of the lawn mower out back, and closed her eyes, lying there holding perfectly still in her bed, willing herself to fall back asleep. If she just kept them closed then maybe she could just lie there in suspended animation and she wouldn't have to say or do anything to rattle anybody's chain. She could keep her life the way it was.

But then the sun shook off the clouds, pulling them back like it was determined to lift the sheets off her sticky body, and she threw them off and padded barefoot into the living room in her cotton summer nightie, where she sat on the beige sofa with her hands folded in her lap waiting for Art to come inside from mowing the lawn. It took him forever to finish. He mowed in concentric rectangles, going back over his own tracks, careful not to miss any spots.

He came in frowning and squinting against the darkness of the interior of the house. He was sweaty and she ran some cool tap water into a glass and handed it to him.

He said, "You're still in your nightgown"—disapprovingly.

She said, "Sit down, Art. We need to talk."

He gulped down the water, wiping his chin on the back of his arm. "Jeez," he said. "Can it wait till I shower, at least? I just finished mowing."

And because she was a coward, and she could buy herself another fifteen minutes of her old life she said, "Sure, go right ahead," and sat there in the living room with her bare feet tucked under her, listening to the familiar sound of the water humming in the pipes, and after a few more minutes, Art humming along to the splattering of the shower. Something from an old Broadway musical. He had a nice singing voice, always did. Art liked musicals. The rest of the friends in their crowd, hard-rock lovers, teased him about his musical taste and Art would say, "I don't give a rat's ass what any of you bozos think," but he'd be checking with Paco to make sure his best friend wasn't making fun of him too. And you had to hand it to Paco—he never was. Something from a Broadway show. *Wicked?* Louisa wasn't sure. She had always hated musicals. People bursting into song to tell you how they felt—and then dancing around, too, as if singing weren't bad enough.

Finally the sound of the shower stopped, and the glass door banged open and closed, and after a while she heard the monotonous buzz of Art's electric razor, and then, as if reluctantly, her husband came back into the living room, clean shaven, and sank down heavily onto the brown recliner across from her, propping his big beige sneakers on the footrest. There wasn't a single item in the living room that wasn't either beige or brown, she noticed. When Louisa was a kid she had loved bright colors, so Alma had always bought her school dresses the colors of popsicles—lime green and lemon yellow and cherry red. Louisa hadn't worn anything bright like that in years. Art didn't look at her. It seemed like he was avoiding her gaze. Then again, when had he ever really looked at her?

"Art," she said, in her gentlest voice. "We really need to talk."

He didn't take the bait. "*What,*" said Art, checking out the watch on his wrist. A glow-in-the-dark Timex that she'd given him one Christmas. "It's Sunday." Like he needed a watch to tell him what day it was.

"God's day of rest," said Louisa. Why did she always sound so pissed off, she wondered. She didn't even really feel angry anymore. Just tired.

"Can't it wait till tomorrow?" Art was looking fidgety. He was setting his eyes everywhere but on her, his gaze darting around. Or had he always done that, and she had just pretended not to notice? "I've got a load of things to do around the house."

"We should talk about what's going on here," she said. She pulled her nightgown tight over her legs, to cover her knees. She knew Art had never been crazy about her legs. Piano legs, he called them, though not in a mean way. "Between us, I mean," she added.

"Nothing's going on between us," said Art.

"Yeah," said Louisa. "That's what I'm talking about." She let out what felt like the first full breath of her adult life. It always got easier, she realized, once you started. Even jumping out of a tall building probably wasn't so bad once your feet had left the sill. There might even be a feeling of exhilaration when your face first hit the air. Even if you were heading straight down.

"Lou. Don't be so—"

"Nothing's been going on for a long time," Louisa said. "A very long time."

"Not this again," groaned Art. He moved around in the recliner as if he were going to run off, but he stayed put, feet on the footrest, eyes on his feet. Worn sneakers, edged green with the newly mown grass. They both looked at his wide, stained sneakers.

"No, look. It's all right," Louisa said. "We aren't going to fight anymore. But—you know." She held her hands out, helplessly. To prove she wasn't armed and dangerous. "I can't do this anymore." Then, to be clear she added, "It's just over."

Art looked at her blankly. "What's over?"

"All this," she said. She hunched up her knees under the nightgown, and nodded her head around the drab room, hoping that her look encompassed all of it—the newly mown tidy little backyard, the study with the closed door, the garage, the bedroom, all of it. She wasn't even sure she was going to miss any of it. "You know." When he continued staring dumbly at her she said, "*You* know."

"Oh, quit being so dramatic," said Art. He reached down to yank on the recliner lever, to launch himself into an upright position. "It's Sunday. My one day to get things done around the house. I don't have time for this. I've got a million things to do before the week begins all over again."

"Oh, honey," she said. She went over and knelt down by the chair, blocking his way out. Art wouldn't look at her. His lips were tightly pursed. He was gazing over her head, as if his real aim in life was to rise up out of the chair and get to that wall. He had put on so much weight these past years that his old, familiar childhood face was half-buried in layers of fat. There were bags under his eyes. He didn't sleep well; he hadn't slept well in years. Later on Louisa might feel a lot of other things—rage, regret, hopelessness—but right then all she could feel was pity. He might just as well have been one of her troubled teenage boy clients, trying to get by on the right medication. It was almost never as simple as that.

"Hey," she said, just to make Art turn his head and look at her. He did. His mouth was pouting like a sulky baby's.

"The week's not going to begin again," she said.

"Who's gonna stop it?" His pale-gray eyes looked frightened.

"I am, honey." He still looked bewildered, so Louisa shifted her weight, bouncing on her toes to keep from getting stiff. Her body was getting older. They had already started to grow old together. "I'm leaving," she said.

His eyes grew wider, frightened. "Where are you going? What are you talking about? When are you coming back?"

"I'm not coming back. Art. —Honey. Come on, now." She put her hand on his arm, marveling at the softness of his flesh under her touch. He'd never been a tough guy, but when had he gotten so soft? She had no clue. "You know how it is. You know."

"Quit saying that. I don't know anything!"

She sighed and went over to the little coffee table drawer where she'd been hiding his catalogues all morning. They were catalogues of men's underwear. Maybe a dozen catalogues, all alike. Handsome young men, tiny bikinis.

"How much underwear does one man need?" she asked.

He looked furious. "You went through my drawers?" he said. "That's outrageous. It's an invasion of privacy!"

"That's not the point," she said. "The point is, this is who you are." She pointed at the catalogues.

He glanced back and forth between her and the stack of catalogues. "I don't look like any of those guys," he said. "As you perfectly well know."

"Art," she said. "Regular guys don't keep men's underwear catalogues hidden in their drawers. You know that and I know that."

"This is an outrage," Art said. He struggled to sit up, but his own weight pulled him back down. Red-faced, he tried to push himself upright.

Louisa laid a hand on his arm, to keep him from running away. She kept her voice gentle. "Art, honey. You know who you are, and I know who you are. But it's no way to live. Jesus H. Christ. You've tried. God knows, we've both tried."

To her horror, Art's face crumpled up like a piece of paper. She couldn't remember the last time she'd seen her husband cry. Must have been the night of the fire, that long ago. She couldn't even remember if he'd cried way back then. She pictured him standing looking lost on a snowy country road, helplessly waving goodbye. She put her arms around Art, for the first time in a long time, the teddy-bear softness around his middle, the way he always smelled sweet, like doughnuts and deodorant and soap. It was a familiar, comforting smell, even while his tears soaked her neck.

"I'm sorry," he sobbed. They hadn't held each other like this in ages. Her go-to guy. Art. They didn't talk, they just held each other. She knew she might be holding him for the very last time. It made her hang on tighter, but in the end it also helped her let go.

CHAPTER TEN

There was never any doubt in Louisa's mind where she would head next: she'd only ever really had one true home, and that was the tiny house on Ararat Street. Michelle was the one who had first suggested it, back when they first discussed the will. Maybe her younger sister had planted the seed of all of this back then. Louisa had her mother's house to run to, an escape route, and if that Englishman Tom was staying in one corner of it, well, Louisa could tolerate him for a few days. She'd lived with worse for a lot longer. Tom didn't bother her anymore. He was okay, really. Sometimes she almost forgot he was there. When he walked he didn't seem to make a sound. When he did speak, he sounded the way she imagined a badger or an otter might if they tried to talk—some kind of woodland creature warbling. He was thin and small and maybe balding, or just one of those men who shaved their heads early, it was hard to tell. She didn't mind him. He had a long narrow face and prominent temple bones and the only thing remotely Johansson-like about him were those piercing blue eyes, so like her mother's and sister's. Louisa had narrow hazel eyes, just like her dad.

She'd never given a damn about any of the stuff sitting inside her mother's house. What did she want with a bunch of old tea-cups and doorstoppers? She'd split everything fifty-fifty with Art, of course—assuming he did the same for her. But she'd still have to buy out her sister's interest in the house on Ararat. The house wasn't worth much; people didn't want to live on a busy road without any decent sidewalks. Even so it would be a stretch, financially, but Louisa could just about pull it off as long as she got a bank loan approved.

She was all set to drive over to Michelle's house, to sit down and knock out all the grisly details, and she knew her sister would do her best to make it easy for her, she always did, but her car didn't drive her over to her sister's swanky house on the West Side of Worcester. Big surprise there. Instead she headed to the top of Ararat Street, where the road began to straighten, the view she knew best. There was the familiar black river, shimmering in the June sun. Sometimes, even now, she felt like she could see the plumes of smoke still rising up from Indigo Hill.

As children she and Michelle had chased fireflies through the long valley leading up to the slope, glass Mason jars clutched in their hands. Holes punched in the lid by her careful father. How many years did it take for the past to recede fully into the past? How many weeks and months had to drag by before you looked back over your shoulder and your own history wasn't chasing you, breathing fire right on your tail? It seemed to her like she'd started running twenty-five years ago, and she hadn't stopped yet. Some people claimed that every single minute of your life was still going on forever in some parallel universe somewhere else, and Louisa could believe it. She could practically feel it happening sometimes. They said this was what caused the feeling people called déjà vu. And if you really stored every single living memory deep inside your brain cells, the way the scientists had proven, then who was to say the universe didn't do the same?

Somewhere in her college notebooks from one of her long-forgotten college classes she'd scribbled down a quote from some German philosopher: "What if some day or night a demon were to steal after you into your loneliest loneliness and say to you, 'This life as you now live it and have lived it, you will have to live once more and innumerable times more.'" *In your loneliest loneliness.* That phrase slayed her.

Louisa wrapped her arms around herself. It had gotten hotter since that morning but she felt cold. She didn't get out of her car. Seemed like almost everything important in her life had happened in or around a steering wheel. Art Wandowski had proposed to her in the front seat of his Ford Escort. She'd ridden to the hospital the night of the fire sitting in the front seat of some stranger's car. Now she gazed up the long slope of Indigo Hill. Had there really once been fields at the bottom, thick with green fireflies? Seemed like she was always chasing something.

It started to rain. As usual. It was always raining or cloudy in Wormtown. Every damn season of the year. That was real; there was nothing otherworldly or déjà vu about that. Just ask Harvey Leonard, the meteorologist. Especially on Sundays. Nothing to do, nowhere to go, and nobody to do it with even if there had been something going on. She was sick and tired of the emptiness. She put the car back in drive and pulled in at the curb by the old Indigo Hill schoolyard, which was deserted as usual. The elementary school had been closed for years. Not to mention she took her own life in her hands every time she tried to park on Ararat Street, with no off-street parking and the cars whizzing by.

Someday, she thought, somebody was going to find a better place to put that monument to those five teenagers who died on Indigo Hill, twenty, almost twenty-five years ago. It was a beautiful monument. But right now the place was overgrown in a tangle of brush, and no one she knew ever went near the schoolyard park—and it had become even more deserted now that the last adult-ed classes had stopped.

Maybe to a stranger the monument was only a slab of stone with some hieroglyphic writing on it. Those names meant something to her.

Each and every name. They stabbed her in the heart every single time. But to any ordinary passerby the memorial might have looked like an abandoned place, a reference to an obscure tragic historical event that most people had forgotten by now, or if they remembered at all, it was just for a second, eyes widening: Oh yeah! I remember that fire on Indigo Hill. By now there had been other tragedies, other fires. That was how it went with every event in history, she supposed—every battle, every catastrophe, every victory.

For Louisa and the Bridge gang, that one explosion had just about wiped them out. She wondered if they'd all still be such inseparable friends if not for that winter fire. Outsiders just didn't get it. They couldn't. Grief and loss drew people tight together in a club nobody ever wanted to join.

Louisa and her friends, the survivors, they still got together week after week, year after year, and while they jabbered about the past all the time—who did what to whom, who got the snot beat out of them in the Kinneywoods back in the day—they almost never talked about the big, central event in their lives, the one that nearly ate out the heart of them, the fire. Paco had saved Flick's life by dragging him out of the shack, pounding out the flames eating their way up Flick's leather jacket. Art Wandowski and Louisa were lucky and had left the party early. Other kids had come and gone that night. In the end, there were still ten left behind inside the crowded little shack . . . Five survived. Five died. It was a terrible thing. But if they had lost track of each other, too, it would have felt like they had abandoned their dead friends to the fire. Then they'd have lost everything. All that suffering would have been for nothing.

The blaze hadn't happened all the way down here by the monument. It had happened maybe half a mile away, up the long hill. If she closed her eyes and pictured it she could still see it—in fact, if someone had blindfolded Louisa in the middle of the night and spun her around five times and steered her off in the wrong direction, like someone playing pin the tail on the donkey, still she believed she could have made her way back sightless over the hills and gullies, through the brambles, up the tear-shaped drumlin by the water tower toward where her friends had built the rickety shack burning in the woods.

It had happened around Christmastime, in the bitter cold. Only December, but they were all of them already sick to death of winter. School was out for two weeks. The kids were done celebrating and opening presents—those who got any—and there was nothing fun left to do. A few of the Bridge gang boys had approached the Jesuit priests and asked if they could maybe use the church rec center to get together and play ping-pong inside someplace warm, but the brothers didn't want a bunch of delinquents hanging around the altar, so they shooed them off. Later, somebody remembered a priest saying, Go take a hike in the woods.

But that's exactly the kind of story people made up later—the way everybody and his brother claimed to have been in the shack earlier that night. Hell, if half the people who claimed to have been inside that shack had actually been there, it would have been as packed as Fenway Park in July.

There were maybe thirty kids in and out all night; never more than about twenty at one time. Kids came drifting in looking for something to do, and trailed back out. Louisa and Art had left maybe fifteen minutes before the oil-drum stove exploded in a consuming sheet of flame. Five unlucky kids perished, and their names were engraved right here on the monument. Carved in light-gray speckled granite. Five lucky kids made it out. The Lundgren twin girl who later moved to Colorado. Paul Bell, who had died at thirty-six from meningitis, Paco, and a younger kid named Roman, and Flick, too—just barely.

At the memory of Flick Bergstrom, Louisa turned her car around and headed a couple of blocks north to his little Cape Cod house on

Brattle. Wherever in the world Flick happened to be, Louisa believed she could have found him with her eyes closed. There were a few stately homes on Brattle Street—but Flick's definitely wasn't one of them. He'd bought his place cheap from one of their old high school buddies, a redhead everyone called Cheetoh. Flick had bought it after Cheetoh's third divorce. He'd left town and crawled off to tan his skin into leather someplace in Nevada. By the time Cheetoh had moved out, he'd pretty well torn up the place, what with one domestic brawl or another, and a couple of wild parties.

There was a gigantic hole left in the middle of the living room, Flick had told her ruefully, where some drunken squid had decided to put in an indoor swimming pool. Flick was handy, and he liked carpentry, so he'd fixed up the little house really nice, at least it looked nice from the outside. He'd painted it a sunny yellow color, added a small square front porch. In summer, now and again he'd grill out on the driveway while everyone stood around the car, yakking, and the girls, as they still called themselves, sat inside Flick's Chevy truck with the air-conditioning on, eating rib-eye steak off paper plates.

Nobody in North Worcester air-conditioned their whole house—nobody she knew did, except her sister Michelle over on the West Side, and that must have been Joe's idea. For people who had supposedly wandered in the desert for forty years, it seemed to her that the Jews couldn't take the heat. Their houses were always chilly in summer and temperate in winter, and in case you never noticed, all their country clubs had extra-strength air-conditioning and numerous swimming pools.

Louisa and the Bridge gang just met up out in public places—diners and places like that. She had been inside of Flick's house maybe twice in her whole life. That sounded crazy, even to her. But it was true. And they were good friends. Really good friends. Though the whole gang got together at least twice a week, every week, and had been doing it now going on almost twenty years, they seldom went inside of each other's houses, except when somebody died and there were sympathy calls to be paid. Then they stood around inside of unfamiliar rooms, suddenly awkward and out of place, while the blood relatives moved about taking trays out of cupboards and pouring stiff drinks into shot glasses no one had ever seen before.

Dropping in at Bergstrom's hardware store was a different thing. It was a public place. That was fine. Louisa went there whenever she needed a mousetrap or a new ice scraper. But Flick Bergstrom's own private house was another matter entirely. She'd driven by and seen Paco's car parked there once in a while—the boys now and then got together to watch some ball game on TV. But never the whole gang at once. They probably wouldn't even have all fit. Louisa stayed far away from Flick's house, and she wasn't sure he had ever come inside hers and Art's place, either.

Louisa and Art weren't big on entertaining. Maybe Art had always felt a little embarrassed about their house; maybe they just weren't all that hospitable. Art always had an excuse about why people shouldn't come over. When Louisa's mom died, they'd held the wake at Nordgren's, like any good Worcester Swedish family, but the after-funeral brunch took place at Michelle's house, because it was roomier and nicer and honestly, because Michelle could afford to pay for that enormous spread.

Now it was a Sunday, and Flick's long black truck sat parked in his driveway. Bergstrom's Hardware was closed on Sundays. Flick wasn't a churchgoer, to say the least; none of them were churchgoing people except for Jean-Marie, who had been raised Catholic and said it was harder to give it up than smoking. She hadn't quit either one yet.

But then, once Louisa was parked outside Flick's house she just sat there listening to the car radio and staring down at her hands. It seemed like a stupid idea, just showing up here out of the blue. Her car's AC blew in her face, making her blink. She wasn't about to ring his doorbell, who did she think was she kidding. And even if she had rung the bell, what was she going to say? Flick, I've been in love with you since kindergarten, and here I am, middle aged and out of shape, now I'm free? Fat chance. The usual predictable love songs were playing on the radio over and over. Katy Perry sang about stealing liquor and not having a clue. A sudden rap came on the window right next to Louisa's head and she practically went through the roof of the car. It was Flick, grinning down at her.

He made a gesture for her to roll her window down so she did. "What's going on, Louey Lou?"

"Not much," she said.

He stuck his head through the open car window and craned his long neck around, as if he expected something to jump out at him and yell, Surprise!

"You okay?" he asked. He had his Bergstrom's baseball cap pulled around to the front, and tugged down, shading his eyes. He squinted at her.

"Not bad not bad," she said automatically.

He shifted the cap forward and back. "I was watching the game," he said.

"Yeah? What game is it?"

He told her. She lost track of what he was telling her two minutes into the explanation. Some ball team she didn't care about was playing some other team she didn't care about it. The truth was, she hated baseball. Most boring game on earth, she thought—next to golf. Golf was like baseball in slow motion, with a smaller ball and a longer, skinnier bat.

"Where's Art?" Flick finally asked.

"Oh. Right," she said. Louisa turned off the engine, and put the keys into her pocketbook. She took a deep breath in and out. It didn't help the drumming of her pulse. If she'd had any sense at all, she would have driven straight to Michelle's house like she had planned, or called Jean-Marie. Meanwhile she just sat there with her mouth open, like she was trying to catch flies.

"Remember Art? —Your husband?" Flick joked.

"Yeah, yeah," she said wearily. "Look, you're going to hear about this sooner or later anyway. Art and I are—well, we're taking a break."

Nothing. Flick's brow crinkled a little, under the cap. When he looked at her uncomprehendingly, Louisa added, "We split up."

Flick yanked the car door open so fast she practically fell out onto the sidewalk. "Get the fuck out," he said. "What do you mean, split up?"

"I think you know," she said in a dry voice. "I think you've done it once or twice yourself." She swung her legs out the door, but she didn't get all the way out of the car. The heat of the summer day hit her in the face and she sank back for a second, blinking against the glare.

"Me, sure. But I'm a screwup," Flick said. "What did you two lovebirds do, have a fight? Everybody fights, Lou. That happens. You've got a hell of a nasty temper."

"No I don't," she snapped. "Fuck off."

He cocked an eyebrow at her. He had thin long eyebrows, surprisingly delicate for such a masculine face.

"I do not have a temper," she snarled, "and we didn't have a fight." She didn't know what else to add. "It's just—look, it's just over."

He put out one gnarled hand and hauled her to her feet. He shut the car door behind her. "You want some coffee?" he said. "I can make it iced."

"Okay," she said. "But I can't stay long." It felt like a magnet was drawing her out of the car, up the front steps onto his screened porch. There she stopped, and sat down on a sagging chaise lounge, covered in an old flowered cushion. She felt suddenly exhausted.

"Wait right here," Flick said. "I'll go get whatever you need. You just wait."

She heard him banging around inside the kitchen. There was a muffled roar rising from his TV set deep inside the house that meant somebody or other on some team had scored a run. She shut her eyes and tried to sink deeper into the shade of the porch. What if somebody drove by and saw her sitting right here for anyone to see? What if Art drove by and spotted her, what would he think?

What do you care what Art thinks, she told herself. Nothing's going on here. Nothing's ever going to *be* going on.

Finally, after what felt like an hour of waiting in the summer heat, when she was stuck to the back of the plastic chair with sweat, when she felt completely stupefied from the humidity of the day and the dull pounding in her head, Flick reappeared, with a tray of the drinks and a bowl of pretzels. He'd even set out some milk for her, in its plastic quart jug, and sugar in an old sugar bowl. Flick always drank his own coffee black and bitter.

He looked grim. "You're serious?" he said. "About you and Art?"

"Like a heart attack," Louisa answered. She added sugar to her iced coffee and a few more splashes of milk till the coffee turned the right shade of brown. Flick made good coffee, but he always made it extra strong.

He sat in the recesses of the porch, out of the sun's reach, on a folding chair made of woven plastic straps. He folded his arms over his skinny chest and shook his head. "Uh-uh-uh," he said. "What'd he do to you? Anything bad? Do I have to go kill my man Art?"

"He didn't do a thing," she said. "You keep your big fat nose out of this, Felix Bergstrom."

"Yeah, I'm glad you don't have a temper," he said.

"I don't want to talk about it," she said—and found to her surprise that it was true. "I'll just go to my mom's old house on Ararat for a while and—"

"Fucking Christ," he said. Then, at the look on her face, he added, "Pardon me." He pushed the bowl of pretzels closer to her. When she shook her head, he started eating them, tossing them into his mouth two and three at a time.

"At least I've got a place to stay," she said. "That's lucky." She realized the truth of it. Lots of people weren't as fortunate as she was. No matter how bad things were, they could always be worse, she heard her mother say in her head.

"Lou, as long as I'm alive you've got a place to stay." Flick slurped at his coffee.

She nodded, too stirred to speak.

"We don't have to talk." Then he shut up, good as his word.

She drank her iced coffee in silence. The only sound was the chiming of ice cubes in the glass, and a few birds calling to each other in the yard. It was peaceful. Nothing that ever lasted. Somebody a few houses down started using their chain saw. Someone else started to mow his lawn. Summer was a noisy time of year. Flick opened his mouth to say something. He had to shout to be heard over the roar of the chain saw.

"You wanna watch the game?" he asked, pointing toward the house.

"Why not," she shouted back.

The early afternoon turned slowly into mid- and late afternoon, which dragged down with it one of those rare, radiant, burning-red gorgeous New England sunsets Worcester displayed just a few times of year. Nothing else anywhere could touch it. They took a few minutes' break from the TV to watch it from the window. Then sunset fell away into a long blue dusk, and the next thing she knew, when Louisa looked outside again it was turning a dark shade of navy blue that seemed almost purple.

"You need some dinner," Flick said, rummaging around in his refrigerator. "You need to keep your strength up." He kept the place surprisingly tidy. He made a couple of thick ham sandwiches, with slices of cucumber on the side, and potato chips and a dish of olives. Louisa was surprised to find she was hungry. They'd watched the first ball game without talking much, mostly to make fun of the lameness of the local car-dealership commercials, and then another game came on playing somewhere else, so they watched that too. In between they played a couple of games of Pitch, both of which Flick won.

By the time the second ball game had gone into its long extra innings—three extra innings, that night—it was almost ten o'clock, and pitch black outside the window. Louisa stood up, suddenly awkward. They'd been watching TV in Flick's bedroom, but it hadn't felt like a bedroom till it turned dark, mostly because they both sat in armchairs to watch. Now she stood next to her chair and was suddenly conscious of his bed in the room, covered by a dark-red coverlet.

"Well, I'd better go," she said. Her hands felt like hammers, hanging at her sides.

He cocked his head. He held still. His face was unreadable. "You could stay," he said.

"What do you mean?" She couldn't even tell what she was feeling—surprised, appalled, offended, delighted? She couldn't catch her breath long enough to say.

He yawned. "It's so late. Believe it or not, I'm usually in bed by now."

"Flick," she said. "Nothing's going to happen. —Between us, I mean."

He peered at her in surprise, then laughed. "Well, no shit," he said. "Jeez, Louise." He shook his head in slow amazement. "You and me, we're buddies. I wouldn't try anything like that on you. Ever."

"All right then," she said. "As long as we're clear on that." Now she didn't know what to feel, either: relieved, disappointed, crushed, offended?

He reached out and poked her stomach. "Come on, now. You know better than that. What do you take me for?"

"You're a guy," she said. She didn't know what she was saying. They were just words, coming out of her mouth randomly, so she didn't just stand there gaping at him.

"I'm not just some guy," said Flick, his jaw tightening, his eyes darkening. Sometimes they were pale-greenish blue. Sometimes, like now, they looked dark green, almost hazel. "I'm Flick. Your Flick."

Her Flick. An inexplicable happiness came over her.

"I just thought you might not want to be alone tonight," Flick said. He patted the big bed for emphasis.

"Yeah, well, you were right about that," she said.

~

Louisa felt like she was an anthropologist, studying a tribe firsthand in some strange culture. You knew someone for close to forty years, you thought you knew them pretty well—but then it turned out there was always something else, something new to discover. Especially if you got the chance to study someone on their own turf. For instance, Flick used the same brand of lavender liquid hand soap she did. She'd never have known that. Or that he bought the kind of toothpaste people with sensitive gums used—though she might have guessed at that, given everything else that was wrong with his body. He went into the bathroom to change, and came out wearing a pair of red plaid cotton pajama bottoms and a Bergstrom's short-sleeved T-shirt, white with dark-blue lettering. "I usually don't wear pajamas," he said, gesturing down at his own lanky body with a rueful expression. She tried not to picture him sleeping in the nude.

They'd gone through a little elaborate back-and-forth argument about how he could sleep just fine on the living-room sofa, but she could tell at a glance that the stiff little sofa was way too short for Flick's long frame. Then Louisa insisted she could sleep on the sofa instead, but he said he wasn't going to have any friend of his sleeping on anything so broken down. "I need new furniture," he said, rubbing his chin. "I keep meaning to go to Rotmans and buy some, and then I keep putting it off. Seems like there's always some better way to spend my money."

"There is," she agreed.

"Like on alimony," he said, pulling a long face.

"Or on beer," she said.

"Yeah, there's that," he admitted.

Finally they agreed they'd both just camp out in Flick's king-size bed, which of course was what she'd really wanted all along, and Louisa was amazed, when they both finally got in under the covers, how natural it seemed, how without awkwardness—like she'd always been sleeping beside him, like she belonged right there.

Flick's bedroom was spare, and somehow calming. She looked at the few items lined on top of his dresser in front of the window—his cell phone, his leather wallet, a colorful glass paperweight, a bottle of glucosamine—trying to memorize everything, just the way it was all lined up, so she could bring it back to mind down the line whenever she needed something to comfort her. She could always conjure up this room. She closed her eyes for a second, to see if maybe she could make time stand still, just by willing it to pause. She wanted to keep living inside this exact minute forever. He got some extra pillows out of the linen closet, and they pulled the pillowcases and the duvet cover on together, like an old married couple. To her amazement, he slept on silky cotton sheets, nice ones, pale blue. She remarked on them.

"Yeah, I know," he said. "Egyptian cotton. That's the kind of thing I spend my money on. Broken-down furniture and elegant sheets."

"I love them," she said, which was as close as she could bring herself to saying that she loved *him.*

"You gotta hear this one song," he said, fishing out his laptop from a little bedside table. Only with Flick, it was never going to be just one song. The man loved music more than anyone else she'd ever known. He always had loved it. At Trivia he could name a song and the band performing it, and the year of its release, all from hearing just the first five or six notes. It was crazy. He took his laptop into bed, and opened it, like he was lifting the lid on a casket of treasure, or raising the sail on a boat, and he played her a selection of songs, with the back of the computer propped against his knees. Flick's taste in music was old school. He played a Peter Gabriel song, "Don't Give Up." Then Leo Kottke, wailing away on a steel-string guitar. An oldie by Frankie Lymon. Not "Why Do Fools Fall in Love," but something she didn't know, called "The ABC's of Love."

"You ever bring girls here?" she asked him.

He shook his head, scrolling through his playlist. She noticed he had all kinds of music on there. Mozart. Opera. Country western. "I live like a monk," he said.

"Fat chance," she scoffed. She was still wearing what she'd been in all day, and she was sure her lipstick had worn off by now, and her under-eye concealer. She must look like hell on wheels.

As if he were reading her mind Flick said, patting her leg, "You're still a fine-looking woman. You won't have any problems. I always liked you best."

"I bet," she said, her heart leaping up. She looked down at her hands. There was her wedding ring, circling the fourth finger of her left hand. Yellow gold, with scrollwork along the edges. She remembered buying it at Sharfmans with Art all those years ago. He refused to buy one, said he thought rings looked silly on a man. She sighed.

"You scared of the celibate life?" Flick asked, nudging her.

"No," she said.

He laughed. "You should've thought of that before. Not going to be so easy. Right?"

"Right," she said. "So. What else you got?" she asked, pointing at the ridiculously long playlist on his computer screen.

"This is so nice," he said. "I forgot how nice it is, just lying close to another human being."

"Me too," she said.

His long narrow face turned toward her. "What do you mean?"

"Oh, separate bedrooms . . . Art snores," she said. "He claims I snore. Probably true."

"Well if you *both* do—" he said.

"You'd think so, wouldn't you?" She rubbed her hand up and down the fitted sheet. She'd have to take a peek later on and find out what brand it was. She never even knew cotton could feel that silky.

"Yeah, the Georgia Peach claimed I snored," he said. "Said it was because I'd put on some weight. So I lost ten pounds, thinking that would make a difference. She just wanted me out of the room."

"Yeah," she said. "I hear you." After a minute she added, "We've been living like that for a while."

"You?" He took a moment to absorb this, shaking his head. *"Damn,"* he said.

"Don't repeat that," she said. "Not even to Paco, Okay? —Maybe especially not to Paco," she added.

"Let me guess," he said. "You don't want to talk about that either."

"Just promise you'll keep your trap shut." Her voice sounded harsher than she meant. That was always the way between them. She was so gruff with him because she could hardly stand how she felt about him, still, after all this time. Her Flick.

"Scout's honor," he said. He reached over and rubbed his hand up and down her bare arm, under the sleeve of her loose-fitting T-shirt, just up to the elbow, sliding back down to her wrist.

A thrill ran through her whole body. That one touch told her everything she'd ever wanted to know about him. Lucky Georgia Peach, she thought. "You getting sleepy?" he asked.

"Yeah," she said. "Let's get some shut-eye."

~

Before he fell asleep, they talked awhile aimlessly about this and that, into the dark. Mostly remembering the old neighborhood, Tommy the Chicken, the corner candy store, some of the crazy stuff they had done as kids. They could always make each other laugh. Her father used to say he could tell when Louisa was on the phone with Flick; no one else made her laugh so hard.

One hour rolled into the next. Flick's profile in the dark looked like a stranger's face, a statue; like a face she was dreaming about, not a real person's. She had to keep reminding herself it was Flick. Flick, there beside her, his voice rumbling into the dark. She told him a few things she'd never told anyone about the night of the fire. Not all of them. He told a few of his own secrets. Not all of them, no doubt. He'd gone crazy after he got out of the hospital. Turned out after all those months, he'd gotten addicted to the pain pills. He'd once tried to hijack a bus. Luckily, the local cops knew him, so they took him to the loony bin instead of to jail.

Then he went back to talking about their childhoods, their favorite first-grade teacher, Mrs. Brown with the soft small hands, playing the piano. Louisa settled deeper into the pillows. A high white moon shone like a man's pale forehead through the bedroom window, behind a stand of pines. Louisa put her palms on either side of her, to feel the silkiness of his sheets. A few small clouds sailed overhead. She was sure she would remember these peaceful, happy minutes into the halls of eternity, surely she would take his secrets with her into the grave, not because they were so important, but just because they had come from him to her.

After he finally stopped talking, after his breathing slowed and grew long and even with the breath of sleep, Louisa sat awake in bed, still, propped against his pillows in the dark bedroom after one o'clock, after two in the morning, almost three, just listening to Flick breathe. She didn't want to fall asleep and miss a single minute of this night. She could tell herself it was the last time but it wasn't just the last time—it was the only time. She was pretty sure of that. They would each live alone. He needed her as much as she needed him, but none of that was any use. None of it mattered. If they both hadn't been such blind stubborn messed-up fools as kids they could have had this happiness together, this contentedness, the ebb and flow of silence and conversation, every day and night of their lives. The moon rose even higher through the pines, three-quarters full and white as frosting.

After a while Louisa could make out the jagged shapes of the dark woods behind his slice of Brattle Street—Bovenzi Park, part of the county's conservation property—sharply outlined by the moonlight. Moonlight poured over half of Flick's face, his skin puckered by scarring. She was tempted to run her fingers over the long jagged scar, but that just wouldn't have been right—and what if he woke up, and she was sitting there running her hands all over his face. Instead her hand hovered over him, like she was blessing him, close enough to feel the warmth of his breath on her palm. Flick did snore, that was the truth. It was a light sound, uneven and raspy, like his speaking voice. It was soothing, Louisa thought, like a white-noise machine; the Georgia Peach must have been out of her ever-loving, flipping mind. Flick slept on his back. Moonlight dripped its liquid silver over the tips of the pine trees in back of his property, and the red and white oaks. Beyond lay darker, deeper woods.

Flick had claimed he could see all kinds of wildlife there in Bovenzi Park, including otters, beaver, wild turkeys, and bear. "A moose moved in not too long ago," he had told her. But she never knew when to believe his crazy stories.

Louisa finally drifted off, despite her best efforts to stay awake. She woke up to the sound of coyotes—she was sure that was real, because her mother had told her about hearing the same howling on Ararat, and about a neighbor's small dog ending up as coyote dinner a few years back. The howl sounded unearthly.

Flick had thrown one long leg across hers. It was surprisingly heavy. His head tilted against hers. His soft hair was against her cheek, soft, like the down on a baby chick. The coyote sounded like a dog, yipping and barking in the distance, but then its howl rose almost to a shriek, and sure didn't sound like any dog she'd ever heard. She shivered in the air-conditioning—Flick had cranked it up—and eased herself out from under Flick's bony leg so she could peek out the window. The sky was indigo blue. Sure enough, there was something trotting across the lawn just then, but the something was too small and quick to be a coyote.

She might have thought it was a neighborhood dog, but the fur was a bright reddish auburn, the shade of autumn leaves. Fox, she thought, but she couldn't be sure. The red fox or whatever it was, turned its head and seemed to stare directly up at her. It held as still as someone posing for a photograph, chest high, bright eyes gleaming spookily. Then, with a flash of its tail, it was gone, and morning had come with a searing grayish-white light through the blinds and Flick was poking her in the side saying, "Hey sleepyhead. You want breakfast or not?"

She threw one arm over her eyes. "Don't look at me," she commanded. She crawled out of bed and locked herself in his bathroom, wondering desperately why she wasn't the kind of woman who hauled a makeup kit around. She was lucky if she remembered to toss a lipstick into her purse, and anyway, her purse was downstairs, along with her keys and her cell phone, which had probably run out of battery overnight.

"You want scrambled eggs?" Flick called from the hall.

"Yes," she said, not because she was hungry, just to extend this time between the two of them, which, she was pretty sure in her heart of hearts, would never come again in this or any other life. *Your Flick. I always liked you best.* She already had those two phrases memorized.

Night and morning were two different animals. By day there was no sharing of secrets, no lying close under his arm—hadn't he thrown his arm across her at some point during the night? Had she imagined it? Or was it just his heavy leg? She could no longer remember for sure. They talked about ordinary things. Flick complained about how much the banks charged the independent stores like his a fortune just for running a customer's credit card. The big chains got all kinds of breaks, but not the little guys. She complained about Brandi at her office, but half-heartedly. It felt like she barely remembered who Brandi even was anymore or why the office manager had ever bothered her. Her old life felt a thousand miles away and a million years ago. Even her twenty years of married life with Art was receding fast, like scenery glimpsed in the rearview mirror.

Okay, she told herself at the end of the meal. Now stand up, say thank you and walk out that door.

She stood slowly, reaching for her pocketbook, which was still hanging over the back of a kitchen chair. "Well," she said. "Thanks."

"One night down, ten or fifteen thousand more to go," he said. He opened his arms for a hug. Flick was a great hugger, even when he was a little kid. He used to hug his mother goodbye every morning when she dropped him off, and then he'd hug their kindergarten teacher goodbye when the last bell rang. Jeez. No wonder everybody always loved him. She rested her face against his thin chest, breathing in, wishing she could bottle the clean clear smell of him and keep it with her forever. His bony chin dug into the top of her skull while he squeezed his arms around her shoulders.

"Hey," he said. "You're gonna be fine, Louey Lou. We got your back."

If she didn't let go right now, she thought, she might hang on to him like a child clinging, wailing if he tried to dislodge her. Nope. Better to be the first to leave. She wriggled free of his arms.

"Thanks for everything," she said.

"Oh, you know," he said, rubbing one hand through his downy hair. "People who love each other should get to spend at least one night together."

They looked at each other for a minute. His lips quirked up in a sort of half smile. He still hadn't kissed her. He might never kiss her. Probably almost certainly not. But she couldn't be greedy, not at a moment like this. "You're right," she said, and sailed out the door, into her new, free, terrifying life.

CHAPTER ELEVEN

"So the thing is," Michelle said awkwardly, "we all agreed I should talk to you about it first."

It sounded to Tom like another stalling tactic. These Americans. They weren't about to let him go home to England, back to Cornwall, the only corner of the earth where he still partway belonged. Michelle was making all the classic moves—digging the toe of her sneaker into the floor, crossing her arms over her chest, avoiding his eyes. Tom however had booked his ticket home, two days forward, and he was determined to be on that flight, come hell or high water.

Actually, Michelle was lying to him and she knew it. They had not "all agreed" to this. Louisa was adamantly opposed to her plan.

"Finders keepers," she'd said flatly, and when Michelle disagreed Louisa finally flung up her hands in a hissy fit and said "Fine! —But I'm not telling Art about this one!" before flouncing away.

Michelle knew things were tougher financially for Louisa now that she and Art had separated. ("Finally!" Sierra remarked. "That guy is gay as a daffodil.") She'd already told Louisa she wouldn't accept a penny for her mother's house, but Michelle knew that still wouldn't make a dent in Louisa's day-to-day expenses. And Louisa had too much foolish pride to take a gift or even a loan of money from her younger sister, which she'd have gladly given.

"I'll be okay," Louisa said stubbornly. They'd had this talk at her mother's kitchen table. On one hand, that made it feel like old times. On the other hand, there was that deep-down sadness. Where was her mother? It felt like she should have been there.

Michelle had poured them both glasses of white wine. She ran one finger around and around the rim of her glass, listening for music that never came.

"I'm sorry about everything. I . . . I want you to know—" Michelle stuttered to a halt. It had never been easy for her to speak from the heart with her big sister. She'd always felt shy, stuck forever in the role of the kid sister. But she forced herself to go on. It was like standing at one end of a rickety log bridge and taking those first wobbly steps into the unknown. "I want you to know that there *will* be a future," she said.

"Oh I know that," said Louisa. "Whether I like it or not."

"No—" said Michelle, still forcing herself to speak. She waited till Louisa had looked up, met her eyes. She was remembering that moment in the doctor's office when the sisters held hands. "I mean . . . a happy one, Lou. A better time. Ahead for you."

Her sister had looked surprised. "Yeah?" she said. A little pleased, a little dubious.

"Yes," Michelle had said—a trifle more emphatically than she felt. She lifted her wineglass. "So here's to the future." They clinked glasses.

You couldn't start any kind of future on a lie, not even a lie of omission, so Michelle had determined to talk to Tom.

"Whatcha?" said Tom now, tapping his foot. "I've loads to do." This was not strictly true either. They were close to finished clearing out the old woman's house. While he and Louisa managed to stay out of each other's way, he still felt strangely displaced with another woman sleeping under the same roof. Awkward, is what it was. As for the rest of the mess, it was on them now. He could clean up the evidence of the past, but he couldn't change it. Time to budge on.

"Well, here's the thing," said Michelle, still staring down. "So. — Here it is. You gave Sierra a few painted plates . . ."

"Right," said Tom. "She's welcome to them." But his senses had suddenly become alert, as if they had all sharpened at once.

"I thought the style looked familiar," said Michelle. "Something about it. And then I turned the plates over and saw the signature. —But I still thought they must only be copies," she went on hurriedly. "Joe thought I'd better bring them to Skinner's for appraisal, in Boston, just to be sure."

"Sure of what," said Tom, with an uneasy feeling starting up in his gut.

"Those turned out to be signed Picasso plates," she said. "Authentic ones. Originals. Apparently a full set is quite rare. And these particular plates were made in a limited edition of one hundred. We think they probably first belonged to my aunt Gritta."

"I see," said Tom. His head was still feeling blank.

"They're worth about $150,000," Michelle said. She was smiling but her eyes looked worried. "That's a lot of money. And they were part of the household—things."

Tom didn't know exactly what that came to in pounds, but he knew it was a lot of money. Enough to wipe out any of Claudia's remaining medical bills, more than enough to buy a new car, since his old Vauxhall Astra was a piece of crap. His mum could finally have a decent vacation somewhere. Lord knew, she deserved one.

"I know you said she could have the plates—" said Michelle, wringing her hands. "But I wouldn't feel comfortable, not telling you what they were worth."

"Well they're mine then, aren't they," said Tom flatly. "I'll take them." His own voice startled him. His own words. He hadn't expected them. Like a stranger was speaking in that cold flat voice.

Michelle's blue eyes widened in surprise, but she hid her shock as best she could. "Of course," she said.

"That's settled then," said Tom, turning away.

~

Tom made arrangements to move back into the chain motel as quickly as possible. He couldn't stay on now at the house on Ararat. He considered changing his plane ticket too, to take himself entirely out of sight, but that smacked of running away and Tom Birch was not a coward. He came down to the lobby and took the box of Picasso plates from Michelle's own hands. Sierra, he noted, did not come along for the delivery. He didn't ask how the young girl had taken the news of her loss, nor did he apologize or make excuses for himself. His rights in the matter were written down in black and white, in contractual legal language. They all knew it. He'd been more than fair, more than generous—but there was after all a limit. And almost £100,000 was considerably beyond his limit.

"Thanks," he said briefly, taking the box from her. It felt surprisingly light.

"You're very welcome," Michelle said, her gaze blue and even. "Thank you for everything you've done for us," she added. "It was a big help." She made a move as if to give him a final farewell hug, but he shrugged, gesturing with the box, to show that his arms were already full, and so she turned instead and walked away. Her summer skirt swayed like a bluebell as she went. The automatic doors of the bland motel lobby hissed open and glided shut behind her.

Upstairs in his room, Tom unpacked the signed Picasso plates. The signatures, in his opinion, were more interesting than the plates themselves, which looked to him sloppy, with geometric shapes painted in muddy colors. He wondered that such naff objects could fetch nearly £100,000. People were daft, was all. Michelle had carefully wrapped each plate individually in bubble wrap and then in several layers of the Worcester *Telegram*. More waste. Tom felt unaccountably angry. He tried to dispose of the newspaper, searching the hotel corridors for a recycling basket—which of course was nowhere to be found. He walked three and a half blocks in the searing American summer's heat with the crumpled papers in his sweaty hands before he found the proper blue baskets with the emblazoned motto, **We Recycle**. That was America, all over, to announce their meager good deeds in large white letters while doing as little as possible to reclaim the world they were busy tearing down.

After that errand was over, Tom ate his lunch in a diner that served the usual unspeakably bad fare. He hadn't had a decent meal since his feet had touched American soil. Every restaurant he had encountered proffered obscene amounts of sweets and puddings, stacked up in giant lit-up glass displays at the front of the place, as if they were afraid the diners might run away unless they were enticed at the door by monumental cheesecakes, slabs of chocolate brownies, trays loaded with biscuits and traybakes and the like. Though Tom was not normally a coffee drinker he drank a bitter cup with his tuna-fish salad sandwich. Anything was preferable to the watery stuff that passed for tea in this country. The badness of the tea almost seemed enough to justify what he was doing. What a relief it would be to get home to Cornwall and have a decent English cream tea!

For the minute, however, his short remaining time in Worcester hung unexpectedly heavy on his hands. He had not anticipated the hammer blow of a real New England summer, broiling and clammy, supersaturated with both rain and sun. He was used to cool days and cooler nights at the edge of the sea. He'd lately learned about some conservation lands within and around the city of Worcester—more than four hundred acres of them in one city park alone. Now that he was free of all other obligations, he could return at last to his true calling, and see what he might find in these famous New England woods. He'd been reading American nature writers all his life—men like Thoreau, Emerson, Edward Abbey, and John Muir. "The clearest way into the Universe is through a forest wilderness," Muir had written. "There is no forgiveness in nature," declared Ugo Betti. The nature writers were not a cheery lot. Like Tom, they took a dim view of human nature. They did not spare themselves, or anyone else.

"Keep your brain in your head and your head firmly attached to the body," wrote Abbey, the crabbiest of the lot. "The body active and alive, and I promise you this much; I promise you this one sweet victory over our enemies, over those desk-bound men and women with their hearts in a safe deposit box, and their eyes hypnotized by desk calculators. I promise you this; You will outlive the bastards."

Tom nearly laughed out loud considering those lines. He briefly considered the two American sisters Michelle and Louisa, committed to their "desk-bound" lives. It wasn't a kindly laughter, but Abbey had also once noted, "Better a cruel truth than a comfortable delusion."

As Tom entered the Broad Meadow woods, under a scattershot of thin shade, and climbed up the sharpest and least-used path he could find, the thought also crossed the back of his brain like the shadow edge of a knife: Wasn't he also entrusting his own heart to "a safe deposit box"—in fact, hadn't he just inquired at the motel's front desk about the availability of exactly that object? Who among those naturalists he admired would approve of his behavior right now? Who among them ever gave way to avarice and greed?

He shook his head as if to shake off the thought and walked harder, faster, up the steep incline, feeling the familiar ache in his calves, the comforting give of soil under his feet, after days of unremitting pavement.

"I just want what's coming to me," he told himself firmly, but the voice in his head sounded shrill, and worse yet, there was no answering remark in Claudia's soft voice. He waited. What he heard in his head at that minute was—an absence—and then he realized that he'd swerved aside to avoid some bramble bushes and lost the path. He fell off balance. Panic constricted his chest. He swiveled left, then right, reorienting himself. Yes, there was the sun, at about forty-five degrees, just touching the dark-green heart-shaped leaves of a towering redbud. He removed his shoes and socks, since he was accustomed to walking barefoot in the wild, and rolled the socks inside the heels of his shoes as he had done a thousand times back home. Of course no sane human being ever walked along the Cornish strand wearing shoes. But even in the forests of England, Tom spent at least part of his time barefoot. No walk was truly a walk, he believed, unless you felt the earth against your skin. Stones and twigs were simply part of the territory; moss was a positive luxury.

His grandfather had taught him how to set his bare feet down, rolling from the outside of his foot inward, learning to step lightly. His grandfather had called it the "fox walk." You didn't pound the ground with your heels the way most humans did. You kept your head up, alert, and more or less felt your way forward. It was easier to climb barefoot, and if you had to wade across a stream, you didn't need to worry about squashing around for hours in leaky shoes.

Tom walked on aimlessly, forcing himself to move more slowly. His mind kept wandering off. He had lately fallen into a city gait; rushing past buildings, hurrying from room to room. He shut his eyes for a moment, feeling the sunlight touching his eyelids. He listened for the usual sounds: the rustlings and creaks and bird whistles. He was conscious of the sharp whine of cars and vans from the nearby carriageway. A woodpecker startled him, as if it had beaten a hollow drum just next to his head, and Tom lurched off balance again and stepped down flat on a grasshopper, bringing his weight awkwardly down and killing it instantly. He had fished all his life, and hunted occasionally, with nets and sticks and handmade traps. With his grandfather he had once skinned and eaten an otter. —In all his years of tracking, he had never killed a living thing by accident.

Tom dropped to his knees to study the elegant creature he had destroyed. It had been a long-horned grasshopper, a large beautiful one, nearly seven centimeters long, with two translucent pairs of wings, the shorter pair the flushed pale rose of a speckled lily. Its legs were still folded as if he had murdered a monk at prayer.

Tom rose to his feet. He felt breathless, sick. He headed rapidly back down the steep embankment, almost at a run, heedless of thorns and heat alike. At least now he knew what he had to do. He padded back along hot sticky asphalt he'd come from till he had reached his chain motel, one among thousands of identical motels—where the young woman teetering in her high heels at the front desk gave him an uncertain smile, as if afraid he might pull out a stick of dynamite—and then it took only three or four minutes to get up to his room and back down and he was right back out on the road again, in the brutal heat of the afternoon, his shirt clinging to his back with sweat.

Tom's sense of direction had always been strong, so he didn't hesitate walking out of the downtown area, heading west toward the now-setting sun. That was a blessing; he could almost feel the air cool around him, minute by minute. He walked steadily, aware that his breath was coming more evenly than it had when he was in the woods. His brain felt alive again, firing on all pistons. He carried his burden lightly. He caught the flash of a dragonfly wing hovering over Lake Quinsigamond; the buzz of insects hiding in the frothy nets of Queen Anne's lace growing by the sides of the road. A few miles farther on, a bright-blue butterfly, no bigger than his thumb, the color of a summer sky, settled on a nearby lupine, swaying like a tiny King Kong atop the Empire State Building.

There you go, said Claudia's warm voice in his head. Yes, he was mad as a hatter, but back where he needed to be.

He was sweaty and probably filthy too by the time he arrived at Michelle's broad front door. He rang the bell, suddenly too done in even to raise his fist to knock. Sierra's pale round face appeared briefly behind one of the leaded glass panes at the side of the front door, and just as quickly ducked away, disappearing from view. He couldn't blame her for not wanting to see him. He didn't much care for himself, either. A moment later, the door swung open with a puzzled Michelle standing in the vestibule.

He thrust the box of plates into her arms. "I don't know what the fuck I was thinking," he said. "Here. Take them. They're yours."

He turned and loped straight off, but Michelle set the box down by the door, and ran lightly after him, catching up and tapping him on the back.

"Please don't run away," she said. Her face was as open and kind as ever.

He backed away, smiling, but with both hands raised in the air, as if warding off an attack. "Can't stay," he said. "I'm not civilized. Absolutely. Don't want to be."

"Tom," she said, insisting. "Would you stop for a glass of water?" she asked. "At least?"

He considered that offer. It was a fair trade. He was in fact very thirsty, and it was a long hot walk back to the motel. He nodded.

"Wait here," Michelle said. She ran off on tiptoe, her sneakers squeaking on the boards of the porch, let the screen door bang lightly behind her, and she was back with his glass of water in less than a minute. Mercifully, she had not dropped ice cubes into his drink, as most Americans felt compelled to do.

She stood with one hand resting on the ball of the white balustrade, watching while he tipped the glass back and drank.

"You're sure about those?" she asked, gesturing inside, toward the plates he assumed.

He nodded and wiped his mouth. "Please," he said. "Let's not." Her forehead wrinkled, the characteristic two worry lines appeared between her eyes. "Yes. Completely bloody sure. Could not be more positive." He handed her back the empty water glass.

"Really?" she said.

"I was an absolute prick," he said. "No excuse for what I did."

"Do you want to come inside and tell Sierra yourself?" she asked.

"No!" he said. He softened his voice as best he could. "You tell her for me. You'll have the words. What the fuck-all was I thinking? Lost track of myself. I plead insanity. You tell her that."

"All right," she said. The corners of her mouth quirked in a half smile. "I'll tell her." She held up one hand, preventing him from bolting. "—But can I ask you one more question?"

She must have seen the exasperation in his face, but he nodded curtly. He owed her that much. She gestured at his bare and filthy feet.

"What happened to your shoes?" she asked.

~

Michelle called, a few hours later, to make sure he'd made it back to the motel in one piece. He assured her that he had.

"Sierra all right?" he asked.

She hesitated. He felt the silence before her words. "She went to bed early," Michelle said.

Tom glanced at the clock on the motel bedside table. "Before nine o'clock?" he asked.

"I know," she said. "Teenagers are unpredictable." The silence continued till she thanked him again twice, and they hung up.

Late that night, in the middle of a deep dreamless sleep, Tom heard an animal prowling softly around his room. It was a familiar sensation after all his years of living with Claudia. They'd never had a whole bed just to themselves. Always a stray dog or two curled up at their feet, cats pouncing on and off the bed, damaged creatures wandering through the cottage needing to be nursed. His first thought was of Sasha, a rescue dog that had gone blind in one eye. She had a special fondness for edging up under Tom's legs at night and licking his bare feet. Tom lay in the pitch-dark listening for the familiar sound of the dog's even breathing. What he felt instead was a prickling feeling of dread.

In one bound he was awake and upright in the motel bed (too soft, too many pillows) aware that he was alone, and in America. What had awakened him?

He looked at the bedside motel electric clock with its enormous red numbers glowing in the dark, fierce as a set of eyes. It was *3:13 a.m.* "Christ's sake," Tom said aloud. He had a sick feeling churning in the pit of his stomach, which he tried to push away with his logical mind. That part of the brain, he'd found, didn't function terribly well in the middle of the night; instead the reptilian brain took over, urging him to run away as fast as possible, to get out, get help, *do something!*

This last bit came to him in Claudia's voice, edged with a panic he'd not heard while she was alive and physically present. Could be he was finally losing his mind, here in this American motel room.

"What is it I'm supposed to do?" he asked the darkness.

The sound of his own voice bouncing back from the papered wall made him feel foolish and he lay back down.

Get up, you git! the voice answered. *Now!*

He groaned awake, smacking his forehead with his hand. "I gave back the bloody Picasso plates," he said. "What more do you bleeding want?" He pulled the slick covers over his head, as if to block out the sound of her answer. But no other words came. A chilling quiet fell around him, like fog. Then he had it, with a cold, sickening awareness. That was exactly what was wrong—the eerie absence of noise where there should have been—something. At least the faintest hum of some machine. A hollow dark swooped in across the silence, swift as a hawk. He thought at once of Sierra. The teenager going to bed before dark, the silence he had heard at her mother's end of the line.

Tom threw back the covers and stood barefoot on the wall-to-wall carpet. His legs trembled. He cocked his head, the better to listen. The faint drone of the air conditioner made its steady sound here in the motel room. All right then, there was a sound, so everything should be all right but he could not shake off the feeling of panic. The cooled air created almost visible crests around him, as if he'd been standing in the middle of an icy lake.

What he was straining to hear was farther off by miles. He could almost picture the exact distance between his motel and Michelle's house. He waited, trying to catch even the faintest echo of the girl's machines. But as pitch-black is said to be the absence of color, he heard a deep-black silence stretching around him. He wanted no part of it, yet it was already here, a part of him.

Tom tugged his cell phone from its charger, cursing aloud, and blinked at it. There were no new messages. Michelle had texted to say goodnight around 9:30 p.m. He had meant to delete it. No emergency messages, no calls.

Then everything is fine, innit, he told himself. No worries. The feeling of panic did not go away, or even subside. It gripped him harder, till he could actually hear his teeth begin to chatter. Tom pressed Michelle's number, grinding his teeth together. Her phone went straight to voice mail. A chipper voice-mail greeting, telling how important the call was to her. He did not leave a message.

Cursing himself as a bleeding soft-headed eediart, Tom sat on the motel bed and fished out his trousers and sandals. He was moving purely on instinct now. He snapped on the bedside lamp, blinding himself with its fluorescent bulb. He phoned a Worcester taxi company, its number listed on the folded card provided by the motel. Then there was nothing to do but anxiously count the minutes till it came.

The taxi waited in the dark in the motel driveway moments later, small and insubstantial compared to British taxis, painted a vivid headache-inducing yellow. Tom climbed in and gave the West Side Worcester address. The sleepy-looking man who drove the cab was Arabic, and played Arab music, but he had attached two American flags to either side of his car, clearly in an effort to soothe the jumpy

American clientele. He was less chatty than any Cornish taximan would have been, and silently dropped Tom off at the curb on Lenox Street, pointing wordlessly to the dollar amount on the screen beside the steering wheel. Tom paid and got out, his sandals crunching on the Hiatts' long gravel driveway.

He felt both the eeriness and errant stupidity of standing in the middle of the night on a dark and safe and vastly silent American suburban street. Mist swirled around his ankles. The streetlamps wore trembling white halos of fog. One light gleamed from deep within the bowels of Michelle's big house—someone had left a kitchen light on, apparently. There were no other signs of life anywhere, and Tom considered the idea of calling back the cab company, forgetting the whole thing, simply riding back to his motel and going back to sleep. Instead he ran up the porch stairs, brushing past damp wisteria leaves, and his forefinger of its own accord pressed the front doorbell. Almost immediately a light snapped on upstairs. Then another, and he glimpsed Michelle moving along the upstairs hall in a white nightgown. She must have paused out of habit to check Sierra's room.

Within forty seconds came her piercing scream, a man's voice calling, the sound of pounding on a door, and lights flicking on all over the house. Tom shrank back into the shadows. He had simultaneously no idea what was going on inside the house, and a clear vision of what was happening within. His heart went on slamming inside his chest as the minutes ticked by.

The hospital ambulance pulled up surprisingly fast, emergency workers jumping out of three car doors at once, like a clown car in a circus. Their flashing red light splashed the leaves of the yard as if with blood.

Joe came running out the front door first and pounded down the porch stairs with Sierra a deadweight hanging in his arms, wrapped in a pink blanket. Michelle raced just behind, a pair of jeans thrown on under her nightgown, her blonde hair crushed to one side from sleep.

The medics lowered the girl onto some kind of cot, talking to her all the while, strapped her down, and wheeled her into the back of the ambulance. At least she must be still alive then, Tom thought. Her father tried to climb in after her but was signaled to wait. Michelle stood with her hand over her mouth like someone watching a horror movie. Her gaze barely flicked over Tom's figure; then she blinked and seemed to come to awareness that he was in fact standing there.

"Did Sierra call you?" Michelle asked hoarsely. Her hand was still covering her mouth as she spoke.

"No," said Tom.

"But you rang the front doorbell?"

"Yes."

She came a few steps closer and gripped his arms, shaking him slightly. "Then how did you know?"

He shook his head helplessly. He couldn't describe the silence at her end of the phone, the prickling intuition, the nightmare of the prowling animal. He could never explain these things. "Is she all right?"

"She turned off her insulin pump," said Michelle in a choking voice. "It's been off all night." At a signal from one of the EMS workers, she dove inside the open door of the ambulance.

Joe pushed in next to her, grim eyed, hatless, not a hint of his usual calm good humor. Both twisted around to the back to face their child. The medics finished whatever they were doing and jumped back into the van. All the car doors slammed closed at once.

The emergency vehicle pulled out into the night, gravel spurting under its wheels. The siren sliced into the silence, as if cutting a path forward. Its crimson taillights appeared to wobble and sway as it set off down the street but that, thought Tom, was only a trick of the light.

CHAPTER TWELVE

A few days later, Tom stood pacing in the same long driveway on Lenox Street. This however was a calmer pacing, or as calm as an impatient man could get. He had lived a dozen more lifetimes in the space of those days—first the anxiety and then the girl's medical reports that trickled down to him with infinite slowness, and finally the good news. They'd caught her early enough, earlier than most, the doctors told the family, and an unthinking intern had added that she wasn't the first teenager who'd tried shutting down. Now they were going for a simple nature walk: mother, daughter, Tom.

Michelle had dressed for a climb to the top of Mount Everest, her daughter for a day at the beach, in too-short denim shorts with a ragged hem and cheap rubber flip-flops on her feet. Neither had thought to pack so much as a thermos of water.

Tom sent them back inside to change into something sensible, and filled the water bottles while he waited. He told Michelle to shed the hooded sweatshirt—it was coolish now, but would become increasingly hot as the sun rose higher, and to reconsider her heavy socks. He ordered Sierra to don long sleeves, long pants, and a sun hat.

"I don't wear hats!" said Sierra with disgust. She acted as if he'd told her to put on a clown wig.

"Wear one of your da's caps," ordered Tom.

Tom had changed his plane tickets home for the third and, he hoped, final time. It was absurd. He could have crisscrossed the ocean several times for all the pounds they were charging him in change fees—but never mind all that, he thought. Let it be. His cottage back in Falmouth was bought and paid for. The medical bills would soon be sorted out. (Thank God he didn't live in America. Barbarians.) He still worked and made a good wage. His mum was pensioned for life. All right, then, plane tickets. Where else would he spend his money now? He supposed he'd distribute it with donations to various worthy charities. Just the idea of making out all the checks and mailing out the envelopes made him feel knackered.

"Don't you have a decent pair of hiking shoes?" Tom asked the girl. "Something waterproof, with treads?"

Sierra laughed right in his face. "That's all I'd need," she said. "Freak out." She made some gesture with her fingers that looked like a victory sign.

Michelle appraised her daughter. "You still have your good sneakers, don't you? The ones you use for gym?"

Sierra rolled her eyes. "I guess," she said—but without the usual sneer. She'd been remarkably pleasant and cooperative ever since the night of the ambulance. Very deliberately so. She smiled more, Tom noticed, and said please and thank you, and when she thought no one was looking she had a hunched, guilty look—but at least not a furtive one. That would have been more troublesome, and greater reason for worry. Her parents had put her into counseling at once, of course, then jumped in after her with both feet. Tom wouldn't be surprised if their dog now had a therapist, as well.

Sierra had stopped rimming her eyes in kohl black, and Tom thought he could detect a shining brownish-gold ring of color gilding the roots of her hair, her natural color coming in under the shoe-polish dye. Those simple things were enough to bring out the girl's real resemblance to her mother. She'd be a pretty woman one day; probably a mother with three or four children of her own, to give *her* heart failure in the middle of a summer's night. And serve her right, Tom thought matter-of-factly. What goes around comes around.

He made sure the water bottles were full enough. They were too heavy, of course, not made for hiking, but he would carry their containers in his own backpack. Sierra and Michelle showed up again downstairs after another slow twenty minutes. In the end he had spent the vast majority of his time in the States just waiting around. Hurry up and wait, it was called. How long did it take a pair of human beings to change a pair of bloody *socks*? They were rapidly losing the early morning light. He supposed most men spent at least half their lives waiting by the door for some woman or other.

Sierra lifted one thermos and sniffed at it suspiciously. "Tap water," she said, turning to her mom for help.

Michelle laughed and poured the water out into the sink. "We only use the tap for watering plants and bathing," she said. "Joe insists on our having filtered water."

"Because the pharmaceuticals are, like, just pouring all these dangerous chemicals into the Massachusetts reservoirs," said Sierra. "Plus the water tastes like crap."

"Joe has handled a few cases," said Michelle more cautiously.

"Did you know some of our county water pipes date back to the 1800s?" Sierra said. "Talk about *old* materials. Time to crack open the wallet, folks!"

"Sierra put together a project on water conservation last year," said Michelle, fluttering one hand lightly down on her daughter's shoulder. She touched her as if afraid the girl might break, or run away—or shake her off, more likely, thought Tom. "She won an award for it."

Sierra grinned one of her rare grins, which made her round cheekbones rise. "Yeah, it didn't completely suck," she agreed.

Michelle poured water from a thin chrome spigot attached to the door of the refrigerator. "Filtered," she explained. Tom watched in fascination. You had to hand it to the Americans when it came to ingenuity and gadgets.

The initial invitation to go for a ramble had been issued from Tom to Sierra alone—atonement for the stupid bloody mistake with the plates—but Michelle had immediately included herself, and Tom was fine with that. The walk into nature might be slower, but at least there'd be no awkward lapses in the conversation with the mother around. If she wanted to attach the girl to her hip, it would have been understandable. Not pleasant, of course, but a reasonable response—or as near as anything to do with being a parent could ever seem reasonable. Tom's own mum was more than a little daft when it came down to him.

He had often wondered, with genuine amazement each and every time: Why did human beings indiscriminately worship their own sons and daughters, while remaining unmoved by the deaths of other people's children? Not all species cared for their young; quite a few ate them. Tom had no offspring, he had been spared that much at least; to him it was all a mystery. If only there were some way to harness that particular and narrow wellspring of human loving-kindness, and spread it out across the board. A little more for everyone. Not quite so much focused in one very narrow, scalding beam.

Getting Michelle and Sierra out to the car and settled in was like herding cats. One or the other kept swerving away and heading back to the house for something forgotten: an umbrella (the sun was shining); antibug spray; an extra tube of sunscreen; some snacks for the car ride (ten more minutes) and so on. And then, they weren't halfway down Lenox Street itself when Michelle suddenly signaled, pulled over to the curb, and set the car into park.

"Can you drive on the wrong side of the road?" she asked Tom. "Like, here in America?"

"Yes," he said.

"You sure?" she pressed him.

"Are you feeling all right?" he asked. Because now she had one hand on the door handle of the car.

"I'm fine," she said, twisting her head around to regard Sierra, who was leaning forward from the back seat with a worried look. "You two go on ahead without me. Nature walk. Please. I hate nature."

Sierra guffawed.

"I hate bugs," Michelle went on, "and I don't enjoy wearing sunscreen, and I'm not fond of long hot walks, either. You two go on ahead and have fun." She opened the car door and slid out. Then she bent and peered back in at Sierra.

"You good without me?" she asked her daughter.

"Yeah, Mom," said Sierra in a bored voice, trying not to look chuffed. "I don't actually need a chaperone every time I leave the house."

"I'm aware of that," said Michelle in a slightly aggrieved voice.

No one, of course, had consulted Tom about any of this. He slid into the driver's seat, feeling the strangeness of sitting on the wrong side of the car whilst holding a steering wheel. His hands immediately began to sweat. "Brilliant," he said aloud, to be reassuring. Chiefly to reassure himself. "Brilliant," he repeated.

Michelle closed the car door on his side. She had left the window partway open, and he had no idea how to close the thing. He adjusted the rearview mirror. He swallowed.

"You'll be fine," a voice whispered in his head. He thought it was Claudia's, then realized Sierra had leaned forward to say it.

"Right," he said, hitting the wheel for emphasis. The car horn let out a honking blast, startling all of them.

"Coming up front," Sierra said, scrambling over the top of the back seat. She made a great show of fastening her seat belt while Michelle looked on, trying her best not to appear terrified. "Okay," Michelle said. "We're all okay." She stepped back from the car.

Once settled in, Sierra said to Tom, "Right. Gun it."

He pulled slowly away from the curb. He felt the car wobbling under his touch, like a bicycle.

"Don't forget to check for ticks!" Michelle called after the car. "And use bug spray! Reapply it every sixty minutes."

Tom kept on driving.

Sierra yanked down the sun visor, slid a panel sideways to peer into a small rectangular mirror, and smiled at herself. "Brilliant," she said.

~

Sierra was a quick learner about moving around in the natural world. Tom was impressed. It wasn't an easy talent, that one. Tom suspected it was inborn. Not that Sierra made a big show of it. She was as fastidious about noting the differences between bark and leaf patterns as she'd been about organizing her grandmother's silverware. She even took notes on her small pink cell phone. He'd nearly told her to leave the cell phone to fry in the hot car, but she had muted it on her own and now he was glad he hadn't imposed any rules on this hike. Mostly the gadget rode in her hip pocket, and she wasn't always staring down at the screen, for a change.

He started her off with the most basic things, like walking softly instead of pounding around, finding her own center of balance, and paying attention to where she was going. She took to all of it like a duck to water. If you knew how and where to walk, and you paid close enough attention the rest would eventually follow. He showed the girl how to place her feet so as to barely stir the dust under her heels. He demonstrated how to balance her body's weight on zero degrees of difference, not splay-footed the way urban walkers typically plodded along; holding herself upright so that both arms were free and loose, and she could look around and respond to things quickly.

Balance, he explained, was another sense, just like sight or taste or smell. If you held your center of gravity properly you could move at whatever pace you liked, and you wouldn't grind your heels into the ground, leaving tracks wherever you went and blurring everything else.

Sierra rolled her eyes when Tom made her practice the same few steps over and over, but she got the hang of it faster than most. Much faster, in fact. Then he pointed out a few of the easier animal tracks to follow: duck prints in the mud looking like engraved anchors; the childlike handprints of raccoons. It was a hidden world, right here in her hometown, and her astonishment at it seemed genuine. She let out little exclamations. "Holy Hannah!" and "Oh my word!" She used curious old-lady expressions as she bounced ahead of him. She soon began spotting things on her own.

The danger, as for all beginning trackers, was that she overtrusted her sense of sight. Emerson had once called the American public a giant, ambulant "transparent eyeball." That was an accurate assessment, Tom thought. America's chief exports these days were mostly visuals: advertisements, movies, music videos. Tom had Sierra shut her eyes about a quarter of the way into the park.

Sierra giggled for the first minute or so, just as any kid would, but he taught her how to swivel her head to locate the sounds occurring in the woods. Acorns spattering on the forest floor. Wind soughing through the waxy leaves of the white oak made a different sound from the red oaks, if you paid any attention. Rain would sound different too, he told her, spattering through the lobed leaves; she should try listening sometime.

When he closed his own eyes he could discern the world around him stirring to life. Here, you never entirely lost the sound of automobiles swishing by in the distance. But closer sounds rose up as well. They emerged from behind the usual wall of ambient sound. Squirrels angrily chattering—they misplaced most of the nuts they buried, Tom explained; squirrels were dull as ditch water compared to the common crow.

He had her practice locating the sound of a thrush singing its heart out on a low branch, the bird repeating the same musical phrases over and over, then switching to a new one just when it had it right. This listening exercise was especially good practice since the birds were dun colored, small and dumpy till they flew past you in a blur.

Three red-winged blackbirds chased away a falcon, scolding all the way. He told her to open her eyes and watch them go.

"How do they do it?" she asked in amazement. "He's so much bigger. Why doesn't he just turn around and eat them?"

"The power of community," Tom said. Then, lest he sound preachy—"Or maybe the falcon's just lazy."

On the low branch of a pin oak Tom spotted the first red cardinal he'd ever seen close up, and Sierra teased him for his excitement. "Wow," she said. "Let's call the press."

"The only way a red cardinal ever reaches the UK," Tom explained, "is if they get carried onshore by some tourist with no more sense than to leave the bird behind." There'd only been a handful of sightings on the British Isles, and Tom wasn't one of them. The bird was a beauty. For him, it was the experience of a lifetime. He'd expected to be dazzled by the scarlet feathers but he hadn't been fully prepared for the loveliness of its singing.

"Hear that?" he told her. "The cardinal harmonizes with itself."

"No way."

"Double voice box. —Hear that upsweep?" They listened together.

"Don't you have any birds where you live?" she asked.

"We do," he said. "Just not that one." Cornwall had more than its fair share of feathered creatures, mostly coastal but all sorts, really, from mute swans to kingfishers, ducks, winnards, and kittiwakes. No cardinals, though. And no nightingales, either, he told her, that most British of birds.

"There's a famous poem about a nightingale," she said. "By a poet named John Keats."

She must have thought he was a stupid prat who had never opened a book. "Now more than ever seems it rich to die. To cease upon the midnight with no pain . . ." Yeah, he'd heard about a poet named John Keats.

But Sierra was good at the tracking bit, he'd give her credit for that. She spotted a wild turkey feather from two yards away, and he told her she could take this one away with her, but never to just grab any old stray bird feather or, depending on the species, you might end up behind bars.

"That'd be pretty funny," she said, "after everything I've done—if I ended up in jail over this thing." She waved the long turkey feather at him with a sardonic expression.

But he noticed she hung on to that striped feather like a kid who had won a prize. She ran her finger along the white bars against the bronzy black. Tom told her in many cultures turkey feathers were considered omens of good luck.

"This?" she said, tapping her fingertip against it, but looking pleased.

"A fallen feather is a gift from above," Tom told her. "Course it all depends on what you believe—if you believe in anything. That feather is a part of the bird, it's not just a bit of decor that you run off on a machine or buy and sell in a tourist shop. It represents trust, honor, strength, wisdom, power . . ."

"All that in one turkey feather, huh?" she said. She was looking flushed.

"So they say." He made the girl sit down and rest on a large flat rock. He was afraid Sierra might overexert herself. She was red in the face and seemed a bit out of breath from the climb. He didn't know what symptoms to watch for, exactly. But she refused to plunk herself down till he did. He said nothing, just sat and let the sun warm the top of his skull. A veery trilled at a distance. He relished the quiet for a few minutes.

"You're probably wondering why I tried to off myself," she said.

"No. Not really," he answered.

Sierra grimaced. "Well then, you're the only one in the world who doesn't."

"Right," he said. His stomach sank. He was no good at these kinds of heart-to-heart talks. Best to stick with the nature stuff. More about feathers.

She checked him out, perhaps to see if he actually meant for her to shut up. She was sitting a few feet away, both her sneakered feet flat on the forest floor. He kept his face neutral. He wasn't giving any cues one way or the other. If she needed to talk, well then let her talk.

"I didn't mean to worry anybody," she said. "I was just testing . . . Like putting your foot over the edge of a cliff. It's not that you want to drop. Um, I thought I'd probably just fall asleep and my mom or dad would come find me and turn the pump back on. I mean, maybe that's what I thought—if I was thinking anything at all."

He considered this. "Bollocks," he said.

"What?" Her mouth popped open in surprise.

"Sierra. There probably isn't one single thinking, sane, sentient human being who hasn't ever considered putting an end to it," he said. "But that doesn't necessarily mean you've gone Bodmin. It doesn't make you rotten or untrustworthy. It doesn't mean you're going to do it. Or not do it. But feeling unhappy or disappointed is still not reason enough to throw—" He gestured around them, at the vast green canopy of trees curving overhead. "—all of this away. You quite likely don't get another chance." He sounded angry, but he just felt stupid talking at her like this, like some pillock old priest. "Figure out who you want to be. That's all. It's your life. Don't hand in your ticket before you're ready. And for Christ's sake don't waste it."

Sierra had gone very red in the face. He was afraid she might start crying, and then he wasn't sure what he was supposed to do, exactly.

Drive her home, probably, and try not to kill both of them in an auto smashup. He'd had as much of weeping women as he could stand.

"What if you *do* sometimes—feel—ready?" she asked.

"Well, it isn't all about what you feel either," he said brusquely. "Trust me on that one." He spoke quickly. "Figure out where you want to go in this life. You're not just some bloody puppet. Nor are you in absolute control of everything. You steer halfway between, but it helps if you're aiming at something good. See if you have some job to do. If there's any purpose to your being here at all, a chance you might do the other fellow a bit of good. Then you have to stick it out. And you, you're still green as a leek. You don't even know what a feather's good for."

"Yeah I do," she said. "They're good for flying, duh."

He let out a puff of air. "That's just what I've been on about. We can't take anything for granted. Even feathers are for more than simple flight. Think about insulation and thermodynamics, for a start. The air moving through helps an owl to listen for the movement of its prey. And then the fringed edge of the feather muffles the sound of its own approach; slows it down; lets it fly at two miles an hour when it's gliding in for the kill."

The girl seemed to be still more or less paying attention, and she wasn't crying so he pushed on. "Feathers help keep a bird clean, line their nests, they make fine camouflage. Just look at that wild turkey feather in your hand—the soft dull brown and gray blends in with the woods, innit? Some species can even sing with their wings, did you know that? They make hums and whistles and drumming sounds. Darwin wrote about it long ago, in *On the Origin of the Species*. And if you ever see a woodcock in action—they do something called a sky dance, when they're looking for a mate, right? They rise up high as a five-story building, then drop like a leaf, the wind whistling through its feathers. If a bird can do all that without even half trying, how in the hell do you know what *you* can accomplish?"

"I never said I did know." The girl folded her arms. "It's you grown-ups who pretend to know everything."

"Fair enough," he said with a smile and a shrug.

"Sorry," she mumbled.

"Hey—I was the total prat here," he said. "A complete pig. Over a set of plates I wouldn't even eat off of. It is I who owe you the apology."

She let him hang for a minute, and he didn't blame her. "Okay," she said finally, from under the curtain of hair that fell over her eyes. "Apology accepted."

He pushed on. "I wish you'd never try anything as crap as shutting off your pump again. If you feel tempted, might give a call, yeah?"

She looked at him opaquely for a few seconds. Her eyes were flat and dark, like two blue disks. What was he supposed to do if the teenager called his bluff and said no, she'd keep right on trying to kill herself till she succeeded, he wondered. Fall on his knees and beg her not to do herself in? Come out with some more sentimental tripe about how grand and glorious life was, such an adventure and so on? Drive her out of the woods and back toward home with a stick? He felt his heartbeat jump twice, three times while he waited.

"Yeah," she said. "Okay."

"Yeah?" he said, as if indifferent. He risked adding, "And if you don't reach me, you just call your mum or your dad."

"All right, all right," she said. At a look from him she added, "I *promise* to call one of you, or all three, okay? —In fact, you can give me your number right now."

He dictated the number aloud and Sierra added it into her phone, her thumbs flying madly. Future generations would need to grow an extra pair of thumbs, he mused. He'd once read that men's hands had evolved for punching, women's for dexterity.

"And I'll add my number to your contacts, too. Like, just in case *you* ever need *me*," she put in. He had a feeling this was some essential ritual of friendship for her generation, something like pricking your pinkie fingers with a knife and rubbing the bloody tips together had been in his.

"My phone's in the car but we'll get to it." He rose to his feet, scanning the sky for signs of rain. "We've got almost an hour's walk back." He could not reliably read the weather here. Even the cloud formations in an American sky struck him as obscure. Mysterious place, this young country. He figured it was about the same age as Sierra, more or less. A chav teenager. Cocksure and half-cocked. No wonder it kept throwing its weight around in the world and getting itself into all kinds of trouble.

He stood waiting, biding his time, while Sierra monitored her blood sugar, and ate a few raisins and almonds from her backpack. It was easier to be patient in a forest. They both drank some water. He explained that the best way to carry water was inside your own body. He wanted her to like this place. He wanted her to feel safe here. He'd done enough reading to know that hiking was excellent exercise for diabetics, at least as long as she didn't try anything risky.

As if she was reading his mind Sierra said, "This place is okay. Peaceful. I might even come back here sometime."

"With a mate?"

She looked at him quizzically.

"With friends? —You need other people," Tom added.

She munched musingly on another handful of the dried fruit and nut mixture, picking the peanuts out and tossing them onto the carpet of pine needles around them. "You mean, like in general, or just when I go for a hike?"

"Like both," he said.

By the time he'd driven her back to her big white house—she read him the directions off her cell phone—he was soaked in sweat from the effort of not turning automatically into the wrong lane or steering the car into oncoming traffic. He could have gotten her there blindfolded by foot. A car was a different animal. An American car on back-assward

American roads, something else entirely. He'd never driven an automatic. No one back home drove an automatic unless they were an invalid. He kept looking for the clutch and the gear shifts. Everything in this backward country was bloody backward. Once or twice he came close to sideswiping a car, and to compensate he'd run up onto the shoulder of the road, scraping against branches. Sierra didn't seem to notice. She was back in her own world again, with her da's cap yanked down low over her eyes, and her face aimed into the lit-up screen of her phone. She barely glanced up when he finally bounced with relief into her long gravel driveway and wrestled the damned car into park. The engine felt more like it had coughed and died than it had turned off. He handed the keys over to her.

"Got you home alive," he said.

"I never doubted it," she said, grinning. "You want to come inside, for a cup of tea or something? My mom can drive you back to your place."

"No thanks," he said. "I like to walk. I'll see you tomorrow, yeah?"

"Okay," she answered. She bent and retrieved the long turkey feather from the floor of the car. She studied it again, smoothing the edges with her fingertips. Then her eyes scanned the gray sky. "Looks like it might rain."

"I won't drown," he said. "Not being a turkey, myself."

She looked at him quizzically.

"Turkeys can drown in the rain," he explained. "Noble birds, but not the brightest."

"Okay, then." They both got out of the car, standing on opposite sides of the driveway. The curtain twitched at the living-room window. Michelle, looking out with a worried smile he could read without having to actually see her face.

"In you go," he said, giving a quick wave as he set off. He watched Sierra's small square back march away. Front door opened, and then closed. Only then did he set off for the motel.

She was right about the rain, of course. He got completely soaked on the walk back to the motel.

~

Tom had booked the earliest flight to London available, with a transfer to Falmouth, but he was the sort of flier who traveled light and arrived hours early. That meant he'd checked out of his motel before eight o'clock in the morning, but even so the young woman behind the front desk smiled at him with a mouth that was more lipstick than lips, and asked him to wait a moment, holding up one finger.

"Someone dropped this off for you," she said, handing him a white envelope with just his name, *TOM*, scrawled across the front.

He thanked her, paid his lodging bill in cash and slid the envelope into the zippered compartment of his backpack. It held the same set of laundered socks, underwear, extra trousers, and T-shirts he'd come with. He wore the same khaki-colored foldable fishing hat on his head. He felt no desire to buy any of the grockle-bait that tempted his fellow countrymen, who then paraded around the cobbles of Rugby Road for the rest of their lives as walking advertisements for Disney World, Los Angeles, or New York, New York. None of that merch for him. He might have bought it for Claudia, just for a laugh. But not just to add to his dragon pile. People's anxieties seemed to increase in direct proportion to the swelling of their possessions. He'd come close to selling his own soul for the low, low price of £100,000.

At Logan International Airport, he slipped off his shoes, opened his laptop, and made it through American customs without a hiccup. It wasn't till he was positioned—*sitting* was too kind a word for it—in an uncomfortable bright-colored molded plastic chair at his departure gate, waiting for British Airways to carry him home, that he finally remembered the envelope with his name written across it. When he opened it, a small piece of paper fell out into his lap, along with one other item.

"I knew you'd sneak off," Sierra had written in her big, loopy handwriting. Still a child's handwriting. She drew circles instead of dots over her *i*'s. "I won't promise never to do anything stupid, cause I'm only 16, but I'll be okay. Hope you are too. Thank you. Your friend, Sierra Hiatt."

"Right," said Tom, grinning despite himself. He sat back, stretched his legs out in front of him, and tucked the striped turkey feather safely into the hatband of his hat.

CHAPTER THIRTEEN

Paco, Jean-Marie, Steve, Mary 1 and Mary 2, Sunshine, Dawg, Repeat, Zamboni, and Louisa had all gathered together once again for their semiannual Old-Timer's Feast. They generally held it in the back of the Manor in West Boylston, at a long rectangular table large enough to hold a dozen or more. When they had first started this tradition as snarky high school kids, they called it the Thankless Feast and held it the day after Thanksgiving. Later on, when many of them had spouses and then kids of their own, it got too hard to reliably pull themselves all together at Thanksgiving so they renamed it the Old-Timer's Feast and held it in midsummer. They were still in their twenties then and the idea of ever being old, much less old-timers, seemed laughably far away. Now, in their forties, the name had become almost too close for comfort.

Looking around the table, Louisa noticed that certain members of the Bridge gang were definitely starting to show signs of wear and tear—sagging chins, paunches, crow's feet, hair loss, the whole shebang. The men, especially. Here in central Massachusetts they seemed to age at roughly twice the speed of the women. Or maybe the girls just fought back against time more desperately.

No one had ordered any food yet. Most had glasses of beer sitting in front of them. None of the local fancy craft beers out of Boston for them. They drank what they'd always been drinking: Sam Adams,

Budweiser. A few of her gang drank a six-pack a day, easy. They were sitting around the table, chattering and drinking and kidding each other, waiting on Art and Flick.

Art had balked at the idea of showing up alone and looking like, he said, "a public spectacle" on account of his separation from Louisa. He was sitting this one out. The gang received this latest news in silence. But Flick, of all people, refused to take no for an answer. He'd shown up at the Manor right on time, for a change, and when Louisa explained that Art wasn't coming, Flick did an about-face and headed back out to his truck, tossing over his shoulder, "I'll bring him back, dead or alive."

"Either one's okay with me," said Louisa, but she didn't mean anything by it. Her days were lighter, sadder, longer and—yes, sure, maybe lonelier with Art gone. But she couldn't say she really missed him. Not the way you were supposed to long for a spouse. Not even the way she missed both of her absent parents. Most of the time she felt relieved, as if someone had given her life back. She'd once read in one of those ladies' magazines that the key word for happily married couples was *easy*. Their lives felt easier together than they'd been apart. Louisa was pretty sure that hadn't ever been true of her life with Art, not even in their earliest honeymoon days. Things were never all that smooth between them.

Even their honeymoon night, in fact. Talk about a bad beginning. Art had gotten hammered on a few too many screwdrivers and Louisa spent the wedding night holding a wet washcloth to Art's round forehead while he puked into the heart-shaped toilet. That was after he'd already thrown up all over her white sequined wedding shoes. Just what every girl dreams of.

Louisa once heard of a bridal party that got stuck behind a hearse, but otherwise she'd never heard of a less promising beginning. The marriage had been mostly downhill from there. And she couldn't pretend it was all Art's fault, either.

Soon enough, Flick returned with Art in tow, under the crook of his encircling arm; Art half grinning and half scowling, casting sideways looks at Louisa as if she were the sun and might blind him if he looked directly at her. He'd already lost some weight, she saw. He looked good.

She waved at him. "How's it going?" she said.

He mumbled something inaudible, and chose a seat at the table as far away from her as possible. All right, Louisa thought. Be that way. Paco was recounting the time they had all brought their mothers to the Manor, on Mother's Day, and a couple of the old ladies got stuck inside the elevator. Sunshine's mother started singing hymns, which was when Zamboni's mother began hammering on the elevator walls shouting "Get me the hell out of here!"

The gang took their time over the meal—it seemed like one crazy story always led to the next, then the next one. The time Paco nearly fell off the bridge. The time Flick climbed the water tower with Art's handkerchief on as a blindfold, on a dare. After they'd finally settled up the bill, there was a momentary silence. Flick looked at Louisa quizzically across the table where he sat opposite her. She tried to interpret the look. Did his raised eyebrows mean, Was it okay that I brought Art along? Did it mean anything deeper, some message just for her?

Louisa had done her best not to act like a lovesick teenager after her night at Flick's house. More important, she tried not to *feel* like a lovesick teenager. She had sternly ordered herself not to call Flick, not to initiate contact, and most of all, not to sit by the phone mooning around like a goony fifteen-year-old praying for it to ring. She did just fine on the first two days and failed completely on the third. She cried all that day. Even at work, for Pete's sake. She ate her lunch in the ladies' room of the office at the far end of the building, the grotty one no one ever used, so she could bawl her eyes out, without interruption. Brandi, of all people, offered her a box of Kleenex when she got back to her desk. After the fourth or fifth day, Louisa pretty much gave Flick up as a lost cause. He wasn't going to come chasing after her, that was for sure. What could you do? You just kept going. She still had the precious memory of that night. New bits of it would sometimes come back to her. A single night was a long time when you broke it down hour by hour, minute by minute, and it was all hers. Forever. Like the Fred Astaire song said, you can't take that away from her.

A week later Flick had finally called to see how Louisa was doing, and did she want to go for a walk around the reservoir. The banter between them was light and easy, same as always. He was so familiar. His long-legged strides slowed to match her steps. Once in a while he nudged her with his broad shoulder. They were always going to be friends. That was the bad news. They were always going to be friends. That was the good news, too.

Whatever the tilt of Flick's head and the raised eyebrows across the table might have meant, Art was the one who snagged her on the way out, steering her by the elbow practically into the coatrack by the restroom doors.

"Mind if I talk to you for a minute?" he said.

"Course not," she said, caught off guard. Art hadn't directed any of his conversation toward her during the meal. Not one single word. She'd never even caught him looking her way. She just figured from now on the two of them were going to act like total strangers. They'd exchanged a few emails in the past weeks but it was all business-y stuff, figuring out car insurance and things like that.

They stepped out together into cool, clear air. August in New England was already hungering for fall. The sumac trees blushed bright red, and at night the temperature dropped like a rock the minute the sun went down. But it was still light out—they always ate their feasts early, to get the Early Bird special and beat the crowds. They might not all actually be ancient yet, but they ate surrounded by the old folks in Worcester.

Louisa and Art walked out into a bright-blue New England afternoon, the sky the color of her late mother's eyes. Louisa wished her mother could have been there to see the beautiful day. Alma Johansson had so loved this time of year—she jokingly called it Augtember, and claimed it was her favorite month. She was grateful for it, every single year. "Thanking you!" That was the way her mother got off the phone, calling the words in a singsong. When you lost your mother, no matter how old you were, or how prepared, you felt like an orphan.

Art spotted a bench under some maple trees and headed toward it. He had always walked ahead. Louisa followed. This too was familiar, but not in a comforting way. They both took a seat. He just sat there for a minute, his hands hanging down clasped between his knees. He didn't say anything.

"What's up?" said Louisa.

Art sighed and shook his head.

Louisa watched little black ants crawling around on the pavement. They always looked so aimless to her, aimlessly busy, like Boston commuters.

"What's going on?" she asked after another long silence.

"We made a big mistake," said Art. "I'm telling you, I really think we did."

"Hmm." She couldn't take her eyes off the ants, still scurrying around. "You mean," she said, trying to choose her words carefully, "that we made a mistake breaking up? Or, getting married in the first place?"

He pursed his lips in exasperation. It was an expression she suddenly remembered clearly, and didn't much like. "I mean the separation of course." He articulated each word clearly.

"I don't know about that," said Louisa.

"Well, I do," he said in his stubborn voice. Art had always been good at grinding her down. That's why he always won more battles than he lost. "I know I miss you."

"I miss you too," she said, and added, "—but I don't think that means we made a mistake here, Art. We've been together a long time."

"Twenty-six years," he said. "Come this December."

"That's a long time." She tried to keep her voice noncommittal.

"I don't think we should throw all that away, Louisa." He didn't just look thinner, she realized. He looked older, too, the lines around his mouth more pronounced. He also looked—she didn't know, was there an expression for this?—he looked gayer. He was wearing a light-colored striped shirt, orange and pale blue, with a pale-purple stripe running through it, and new leather loafers. But really, she had no idea how gay people looked. Only on TV. His gestures seemed to her more effeminate, his voice sounded higher. But maybe he'd always looked and talked like that. She thought about all the nights they'd lain together in bed, not talking, not even touching hands. And other nights, kissing each other politely on the mouth, quickly, before heading off into separate rooms. She had no idea what Art remembered, if he remembered everything differently.

"I think you're just scared," she said.

He scowled at her. His eyebrows drew together. "Why should I be scared?" he said. It was his I-am-correct voice. But with a tremor underneath it. "No I'm not. You're wrong. Just listen . . . I simply don't want us to do something—foolish."

She turned sideways, and forced her eyes from the scurrying ants so she could look straight at him. She had certainly loved this man once. She probably loved him still, if push came to shove. But not like a husband and wife love each other—not even the way she loved Flick, helplessly, hopelessly. "Why not?" she asked. "Why not go ahead and do something foolish?"

"Don't be ridiculous," he said.

"For that matter, why not be ridiculous?"

"You chose *me*," Art said. "That very first night. *You* came to *me*. At the shack on Indigo Hill. You asked me to leave with you."

"I know," Louisa conceded in a quiet voice.

"If it hadn't been for that, I'd have probably died in that fire." Art said it bitterly, as if she'd cheated him of something wonderful. "We never should have left Tommy Bell behind."

"I know that too," she said. She couldn't think of anything to add.

"So why, Louisa?—I never did get it. Why'd you come after me in the first place?"

"I don't know," she lied. "I just did. I was a stupid teenager. You were a teenager. Maybe we should give ourselves a break." They fell silent again. She went back to staring at the little black ants crawling around.

"I don't know what to do with myself," Art said. He sounded near tears. "I wander around that house alone, *our* house, and I just don't know what to do next, or where to go."

"You could sell the house," she said. "We never liked it all that much in the first place."

"That's not what I mean, and you know it," said Art.

"Take some cooking lessons," Louisa said. "You always said you wanted to try your hand at gourmet cooking. Piano lessons, too—remember? Only you never could find the time. Why don't you try some of the things you always wanted to do?"

"I don't want to do anything," Art said, slumping down farther. "I don't even want to go to work anymore."

"Maybe you should find another job," Louisa went on, relentlessly. She knew she was sounding hard but she couldn't seem to stop the words from tumbling out. "Find something you actually like to do. Nothing's holding you back now."

"I don't know what I like," he said. He had a hangdog, helpless expression that Louisa knew only too well. Always, in the past, she'd rushed in to help. Only it never did help. He looked so disappointed now. That downturn of the mouth. He'd worn her down with it a hundred, maybe a thousand times, over the past twenty-six years.

"Well, figure it out!" she snapped. She stood up, startling them both. Art was staring at her with his mouth half-open. She stood in front of him with her hands clenched into fists.

"I'm sorry," she said. "I'm honestly very sorry, but this is not my problem. You can do anything you want—you're smart, you're hard-working. You're nice looking enough. You're a capable human being. I'm sorry if you think I cheated you out of dying young. You're going to have to find yourself another plan." She picked her pocketbook up off the ground and threw it over her shoulder. It swung back hard and hit her in the ribs. "I saved your miserable life—now live it!"

CHAPTER FOURTEEN

Here's what she never let herself remember.

It was a bitterly, brutally cold night. The wind blew into Louisa's eyes, it seemed to crawl behind her eyelids, making them sting in the cold. Then the tears froze on her face, ruining her makeup, she was sure. And this was only the end of December. Winter had barely begun. The rest of the frigid season still lay ahead, raised like a sledgehammer, waiting to slam down with its full weight.

Louisa had just turned eighteen, in late November. That didn't amount to much—Massachusetts had recently raised the drinking age back up to twenty-one. So they still had to go on their "tap a Harry" runs: find some older sibling or neighbor who was willing to go out and buy them the booze. It wasn't all that hard. Flick was a champion at finding Harrys. He could charm the birds out of the trees, the adults out of their cars, and the liquor bottles off the package store shelves.

Louisa was set to go to college in Worcester the next year. She'd live at home. Most of her friends at Burncoat High were going to college too, but none of them planned to leave town. They had plenty of colleges to choose from, about ten of them right there in the city. She heard of kids applying to schools in other states. There was always some genius who got into a school like Harvard or Yale, and then the principal and all the parents practically fell down dead over it and they wrote about it in the Worcester *Telegram*. Louisa had decided on Worcester State. Her parents could afford the tuition, and she would save a bundle by living right there in her attic bedroom on Ararat. She'd heard Flick talking about going to Assumption. As long as he was close by, she figured she could deal with anything. Flick had been extra friendly lately, even for him. He and a girl named Jackie had recently called it quits.

Louisa and Flick had had English class together that fall—which Flick hated—so they sat together and Louisa loaned him her notes, and when he gave them back, they were scribbled over with his cartoon drawings and doodles and jokes. She saved those annotated notes in a shoebox she hid at the back of the top shelf in her hideaway attic closet. She'd have died if anyone ever found that old box of memorabilia. It contained everything she'd ever gotten from Flick; from a portrait of the two of them holding hands that he'd drawn in crayon in the second grade, to the most recent English class notes.

She'd saved ticket stubs for concerts they'd been to together (not on a date, just as part of the larger Bridge gang) and receipts from lunches at the Abare Bar & Grill, where, it was rumored, half the workers behind the counter were ex-cons, and they weren't just in there for writing bad checks, either. You complained about your meal, you might wind up at the bottom of Lake Quinsigamond in a pair of cement boots, Flick had warned her. She could never quite tell if he was kidding or not about that kind of stuff.

She'd saved old tickets from movies they'd seen at the Showcase Cinemas and random notes he'd passed Louisa under the table in class. Nothing romantic. A note from fourth grade, in his jagged, little-kid script said only, "Waht's for lunch?" Flick often got his letters jumbled. Some of his mistakes were a hoot. She had also kept a Bergstrom's T-shirt he'd once loaned her and forgot to ask for it back, and a chewed-on yellow pencil that still bore his sharp tooth marks. Sometimes she fitted her mouth over it, tenderly, as if she were trying to play a tiny flute. She even kept a rubber band he'd once shot at her. Crazy stupid stuff. Stuff nobody in their right mind would ever keep.

Louisa took her own sweet time picking out what to wear to the shack that night, the night of the party. Well, it wasn't really even a party. Technically speaking, the Bridge gang didn't throw parties—but at least it gave them all someplace warm to go. It was still the Christmas holidays, more or less, so she could wear her new holiday sweater without feeling stupid—but red would make her stand out, and Louisa didn't want to stand out. She already stood several inches taller than most of her girlfriends, and a few inches taller than some of the high school boys. It made for some pretty awkward moments on the dance floor. Louisa felt gawky in high heels, like a puppet on strings, about to fold over any second—but then, when she wore flats she felt ugly and plain and not at all feminine. If she tried to compensate by putting on makeup, she went too far the other way, and ended up looking like a circus clown.

Michelle, Louisa's younger sister, offered to help Louisa get ready to go out that night. She was very big on being helpful. "I can make you look even more beautiful," Michelle gushed. "We can bring out your wonderful dark eyes!"

Michelle always looked feminine, and her makeup was subtle and perfect—her clear complexion glowed, her bright-blue eyes shone, and she had that long golden hair that all the boys went gaga over. Louisa was the family goose while Michelle the swan glided on by. And the worst part was, Michelle was not only prettier, she was smarter and nicer, too. Even Louisa's dad, who had always been Louisa's biggest fan, would shake his head these days, watching her baby sister and say, "That Michelle sure is something else."

For once in her life Louisa wanted to look special and pretty herself. Just for one night. So she let Michelle tie her hair up in a high ponytail fastened with a sweatband. Michelle applied purple eye shadow—"to bring out your hazel eyes" she explained—and more mascara than Louisa had ever used before. Michelle helped her pick out her outfit, too—complete with chunky boots, and Louisa's new long winter coat with padded shoulders, a Christmas gift from her mom and dad. Michelle marched her big sister downstairs to show off her new look. Then of course when she was done, Michelle acted all sad and wistful that she had no place to go that night.

"Just let me come, this once," said Michelle. None of her own friends were doing anything fun, she said, and her best friend, Crystal, was away for the weekend skiing at Jiminy Peak. "I won't be in the way," Michelle promised.

"Yes you will," said Louisa bluntly.

"I won't, I won't," Michelle wheedled, her blue eyes wide. "I'm so bored."

"Ohhhh—why not take her along?" interceded their mother. She was doing the *Telegram* crossword puzzle in the paper, and with two pencils tucked, one behind each ear, she looked like some kind of crazy woodland creature, in her holiday vest with the pine-cone appliqués all over it.

"Nobody else has to take their kid sister along," Louisa complained, which wasn't exactly true, and not quite a lie, either. None of her friends *had* a kid sister except for Jean-Marie, who was the eldest of ten, so that didn't count. For some reason everybody in the Bridge gang seemed to have kid brothers.

"Pretty please?" said Michelle. "You won't even know I'm there. I'll be quiet as a mouse. Honest!"

"Let Louie be," said her dad, but Louisa could tell he was disappointed in her. He gave her a quick glance before he turned back to his newspaper, flopping it over to read the business news.

"I'll take you next time," Louisa promised. "No matter where I go. Pinkie promise." She would have sworn to anything to get out of the house this one night unencumbered. —If only Michelle had a clue. This wasn't just any ordinary night. It was special. What if this was the one night that Flick got drunk—not too drunk, but just drunk enough—to lean on *her* for a change, and lead Louisa into some remote corner, or outside, into the frosty air. Louisa wouldn't even feel the cold, she thought, if Flick had his long arms around her. He'd even called her earlier that day to make sure she was going to be there at the shack on Indigo Hill.

"You're not going to stand me up, are you?" he teased.

No, she wasn't going to stand him up. Not Flick. Not tonight. She checked her face in the breezeway mirror before she left—her eyes looked bright, her cheeks glowed. "I promise I'll take you with me next time, wherever I go," Louisa told her Michelle, who was still hanging around all sad eyed by the door, and Louisa fled before anyone could say anything else.

~

Except, the party was a bust almost from the start. For one thing, Jean-Marie got grounded at the last minute so Louisa had to climb the long hill toward the water tower alone, trudging up Indigo Hill in the dark and damp cold. Had there ever been fireflies here? Had there really been a summer? It didn't seem possible. She almost wished she'd taken her kid sister along after all. Louisa hated going places alone. She wasn't even sure where the shack *was*, exactly, or how to find it, so she wandered around on the snowy hill lost and freezing, her feet growing number by the minute, trying to find the old road that the water trucks used. By the time she located the right place, her nose was running, and she was sure her makeup was wrecked—and then, inside the shack, Flick was already standing in a corner with his hand flat against the wall, above the shoulder of one of the pretty Lundgren twins, smiling down at the girl like he was going to take a nibble out of her. Louisa had come too late, as usual. So she'd frozen her tail off and walked all that whole way in the snow for no good reason.

It felt hot and airless, almost stifling inside the makeshift shack, after the cold air. The room felt soggy and smelled of cardboard. By the time she got there, the place was crowded, with barely any room to turn around. There was a big oil drum in the middle of the room that served as a makeshift stove, though it seemed mostly to be producing smoke. A few of the younger kids had tagged along, like Nutter and Tommy Bell. They'd just gone into the high school that fall, but they were somebody's neighbor (Nutter) or someone's kid brother (Tommy Bell) so the gang let them stay. Tommy was the genius who had actually built the shack, nailed it together with discarded lumber from Sloane's and pieces left behind on a nearby construction site. He'd even toggled together a set of stairs, so the shack had an upstairs and a down. The upstairs was basically just a crawl-space—no one but a little kid could have actually stood up in there, but still, it was quite an accomplishment.

He'd rigged up the wood-burning stove in an old fifty-five-gallon oil drum. Tommy did lousy in all his academic classes at school, but he was some kind of mechanical genius when it came to building things and would probably end up making more money than the rest of them combined. Every time somebody new walked in, Tommy escorted them around, showing what he'd done, his dark eyes shiny with pride.

That night, in a holiday spirit they'd all been drinking tequila. Tommy claimed he'd gotten a bottle as a Christmas gift from his folks, but no one believed that story. His folks didn't earn enough to spare him a bottle of Pepsi. He must have tapped a Harry somehow. Even the word *tequila* made Louisa feel warmer and more sophisticated—it conjured up advertising posters of tanned blonde girls in bikinis drinking on a nice beach somewhere tropical. Someplace they'd all rather be. Not huddled altogether in a damp makeshift shack in Wormtown, Mass.

Most of the gang were upstairs playing cards, or downstairs jawing or drinking tequila. Other guys from the Bridge gang came and went, and some of them stayed outside the whole time, but the only girls who showed up all night were Louisa and the Lundgren girls. They could have used Michelle there, just to even things out a little. It served her right, Louisa thought, for being so selfish and not letting her baby sister tag along. Nobody was going to do any dancing with just three girls in the room. Nobody was even playing any music so far. Somebody had brought a guitar but it just sat in a corner of the shack, untouched. Louisa had been counting on a dance to get things started with Flick.

He barely budged from in front of that Lundgren girl once Louisa got there, except once in a while to poke at the wet wood sizzling in the oil drum and make disparaging remarks about it, or to get another pour of tequila. He'd hailed Louisa when she first came in—"Hey, Louie Lou!" and waved so hard he almost toppled over onto the Lundgren twin, so it was clear Flick was pretty sauced before Louisa even arrived. As usual, she was too late. When Flick zeroed in on a girl, he seldom lost focus.

When there were more than ten or fifteen of the neighborhood kids in there at one time, they were packed into the tiny shack like sardines, so you had to watch your feet when you walked, and Louisa wondered what would happen if things went south. The place was a powder keg. You couldn't even turn sideways without bumping up against someone. When she mentioned it to Zamboni, though, he just cut her a sardonic look and called her a worrywart. Stupid, was what it was. Let him call her whatever he liked.

Others of the kids from her neighborhood showed up at some point during the night, though only their core group stayed on—Paco and his chubby sidekick Art Wandowski; Zamboni; Paul Bell; plus a couple of the younger kids who had actually built the shack—Paul's kid brother Tommy and a couple of his friends, looking startled and pleased to be in the presence of the tough, popular Swedish Hill high schoolers. Other boys, more acquaintances than friends, came and went, and came and went. Louisa was bored, and she felt like a frown had permanently affixed itself to her face, creasing her forehead. Her head throbbed from the closeness of the room. Every time someone opened the narrow front door, a blast of cold air would smack her in the face and leave her shivering, and in between blasts the smoke made Louisa's eyes water.

She stood as long as she could, but by ten o'clock she had just about given the night up as a lost cause. Some holiday party. The crowd had thinned; only about a dozen of the whole crowd remained. The wet-wood smoke had given her a pounding headache. Flick had finally left the Lundgren twin's vicinity, so apparently they weren't literally glued to each other after all. The Lundgren girl sat across the room in her cherry-red sweater, with her blonde hair glinting by the lantern light, one long jean-clad leg crossed over the other. She was busy flirting with Paul Bell now.

Louisa stood up to look for Flick.

She could picture herself touching him lightly on the back and asking if he wanted to get out of there for a breath of fresh air. Chances were he'd agree. Flick was so restless he pretty much wanted to get out of anywhere as soon as he arrived. This party was winding down, anyway. Soon it would be over. The muscles in Flick's back were long and strong; Louisa could almost feel them under her palm, thinking about it. Then at least they'd have the long walk home in the cold together, to joke around and talk.

Louisa poked her head up into the second floor to find Flick, but there was nobody up there but Paco and a knot of younger kids avidly playing a game of Pitch, clustered around a messy stack of dollar bills in the center of the circle. The little kids looked mesmerized.

Paco was chanting, "Five dollars a game, dollar a set, ten dollars in the hole!" —So he was going to make some money, though he'd probably spend it all treating the younger kids to M&M's or Snickers bars afterward. The card players barely looked up when she stuck her head up into the crawlspace.

"You seen Flick?" Louisa called to Paco.

"Many times," he answered with a drunken grin.

Louisa stepped back downstairs, carefully, because the jerry-rigged steps were rickety. She warmed her hands over the sputtering fire in the oil drum when she suddenly spotted Flick's plaid shirt, in the darkest, farthest corner of the shack. His golden-brown hair glinted in the light from the lantern, only because he was so tall, even sitting down. He was sitting cross-legged—and now Louisa saw that the other Lundgren twin was sitting in his lap, facing him. They were entwined like a pair of snakes, heads moving. Flick was kissing the other girl, and rummaging his long hands through her blonde hair before resting his fingers on the blades of her back. Louisa could almost feel the ache in her own shoulder blades. She snatched up her coat, and grabbed the arm of the first person she saw—dull, chubby Art Wandowski.

"Let's get out of here," she said to him. "I'm freezing."

His eyes widened in surprise, but then he smiled, and nodded, his round cheeks rising. "Okay," he said.

Paul's kid brother Tommy, the builder, who had overheard Louisa said, "It's not cold." He was proud of the oil drum stove he'd made. He was proud of the whole place. And there wasn't all that much he'd ever had to be proud of.

"Yeah it is," Louisa said. "Feel my hands." She thrust them out under his nose. Tommy Bell looked startled, then reached out one hand and touched the top of her cold hand. He acted like it was the one and only time in his life he'd ever touched a girl.

"I've got plenty of cardboard to burn," he said.

"Cardboard's not much use," Art said. "As a heat source."

"Let's *go*," Louisa said, still hanging on to Art's round arm. "Can't we just go?"

"Would you wait ten minutes?" Tommy Bell asked. "I'll walk home with you."

Louisa was still aware of the two figures making out on the floor in the corner. She wished she could force herself to look away. She thought maybe Flick had his hand moving around under the girl's sweater, but she couldn't tell. The only light came from a lantern hanging in the middle of the room, and from the snow shining through the one small window by the door. Louisa wasn't absolutely sure, but she thought maybe she heard Flick moan.

"I'm not waiting," she snapped.

Art shrugged apologetically. "I've got work in the morning," he said to Tommy.

"Okay then," said Tommy Bell, polite as a grown-up. "Thanks for stopping by."

When they left, Tommy was still standing over the fire, with his head cocked, studying the stove like he was puzzling out something.

"That kid's gonna be a millionaire," said Art, as he pulled open the narrow front door. "Did you see the way he rigged up a set of stairs, and everything?" Louisa dropped Art's arm to step sideways into the bitter cold. . No one from inside the shack called after them. Very likely nobody else noticed them go. A handful of kids still hung around outside but they didn't say anything either. The night was black as coal, and full of stars. A half-moon had risen above the tops of the pines. First the fresh air felt good, then in less than a minute it stung her lungs with the bitter cold.

Art took her hand in his plump hand. Apparently he had misunderstood Louisa's invitation. She felt too tired and too disappointed by the way the evening had fizzled out to argue or explain. Let him think what he wanted. She let her hand rest listlessly in his, as Art led her clumsily back down the side of the snowy Indigo Hill, chattering on and on nonstop. Something about his work, something else about ice fishing, going into great and tiresome detail about fishing lures. Something about drilling, something else about the importance of using live bait. She wasn't really paying attention. Her face felt stiff from scowling. Her new wool coat kept her body warm, but her feet, in the chunky boots, were growing steadily wetter and colder till they felt like two huge lumps of ice, impossible to move.

At the bottom of the hill, something made Louisa turn around. She never knew what it was. Maybe it was a flicker of light that caught her eye against all that darkness. Or maybe she was like that woman in the Bible who just had to look back over her shoulder one last time and risk turning into a pillar of salt. At first Louisa thought she was imagining things; then she was sure she saw it: a sharp bright point of light, blinking on and off like a firefly. She stopped walking. She looked again, ducking under the branch of a fir tree to see better. The light at the top of the hill grew bigger and stronger. Then she felt something like a wave of heat, rolling downhill toward them.

"I swear to God," she said in a tight voice. "I think the shack's on fire."

"What?" said Art. He was still talking about ice fishing, and flooding the fields.

The flickering up the hill grew brighter, rose straight up into the sky like a pointing, accusatory finger. Louisa stared at it in horrified fascination, waiting for the vision to go away. She must be imagining things. It was like staring at a crumpled bag on the road that looked like the twisted dead body of an animal, till the wind finally came along and lifted it away. She waited for the wind to blow this thing out, for the fire to disappear. But it didn't go away. Flames leaped up in all directions instead, spreading jaggedly. She ran back uphill toward the shack to get a better look, dragging Art along with her, and at the next bend, the trees opened, like a keyhole, and through that keyhole she saw a column of blackish-orange flame, rising straight up into the sky.

"Holy shit," breathed Art. He squeezed Louisa's hand and tried to pull her away. Her palm felt trapped in a soft, moist cage.

One of the Lundgren girl twins came pounding down the hill past them. Her hair was wild. She wasn't wearing a red sweater so it must have been the other Lundgren girl. "Get help!" she screamed, and fled headlong toward the road.

Art stared after her, his mouth twisted open. His shoulders were hunched. He looked like a frightened rabbit. "What do we do now?" he asked Louisa.

Louisa yanked her hand away and started running wildly back uphill, blindly. She followed the distant flame. Prickers scraped against her, a branch lashed her neck till she bled, but she didn't feel any of it then. Art shouted after her to stop. She no longer noticed that her boots were wet. It felt like she was flying against gravity, pounding uphill. Art stumbled after her, pleading for her to slow down, to come back to safety.

"I don't think this is a good idea!" he gasped, out of breath. "It's too dangerous. We shouldn't go back!" He gestured desperately for her to come back downhill. She could smell the smoke now.

And Flick—Flick was still back there. She ran straight uphill. She ran harder till Art's words were torn away by the wind whistling in her ears. She thought she saw Zamboni running off in his bright-orange sweatshirt, but if so, he was headed the other way, cutting through the woods toward his house. She didn't feel cold anymore, but the freezing air stood like an obstacle in her path, menacing, a physical force as hard as a wall trying to block her way. She pushed on past it, both arms stuck out in front of her, pounding uphill through the pines as fast as she could, jumping over rocks and tree roots. She didn't stumble once. Her stiff legs seemed to know where they needed to go. She let them carry her onward. Two more boys ran past her, coming from the direction of the shack. "Fire!" one of them yelled in a cracking voice. Their faces were so sooty she didn't recognize either one. Neither boy was Flick.

She fought and tore her way uphill till she was suddenly standing at the door of the shack. She could feel the heat of the fire on her face. It was like a scene from a disaster movie or a bad dream. Flames were shooting off the walls. Paco was running up and down in front of the shack yelling, along with Paul Bell, and flames were licking at the roof. The top floor had sagged down onto the bottom floor, so the boys couldn't get the door of the shack open.

"They're gone," Paul said in a ragged voice to Paco. "The smoke got them." He looked like the image of a hanged man, Louisa thought.

His head was nodding forward, his hands hung at his sides, his body slumped forward.

"Shut up and let me think!" shouted Paco. He tugged at his hair with both hands as if he could reach his brains that way.

Then they all heard a loud thumping noise as if something or someone had been thrown against the door. It happened once more. The door shook.

"Open the door!" Louisa screamed, kicking at the wood. "Do something, get him out! Get him out!" Nobody had to tell her Flick was trapped in there. She already knew it.

She yanked at the door but the doorknob wouldn't turn. She pounded on the narrow door till her fists were numb. Paco pushed her out of the way and kicked at a couple of boards beside the door. Art had finally caught up and he stood at a distance, arms hanging helplessly at his sides. Nothing happened till Paco and Paul picked up a log, and smashed into the shack, using it like a battering ram. The boards loosened. They rammed it with the log again and again. Paul Bell was a big kid. He punched a hole through the window with his fist, and then kicked at the loose boards beside the window with his big, steel-toed boots till they splintered. His hand was bleeding but he didn't seem to notice. Paco reached inside and dragged something through, out into the cold. It was Flick. His leather jacket and his hair were on fire. When he landed in the snow, his hair made a sizzling sound. Louisa threw handfuls of snow on his jacket till that went out, too.

Flick's face was red and black, like a mask, but he was awake, alert, and his blue eyes were blazing in his head, still completely alive, still Flick. He picked himself up out of the snow and stumbled forward, his legs rubbery. Paco and Paul grabbed him under either arm, and Louisa followed them. It felt like a scream was stuck in her throat, like the point of a sword.

"Poor Tommy," said Paco, in a broken voice. "He poured gasoline on the fire, to make it warmer. Crazy kid."

Art made a sound.

"I tried to stop him," said Paul. "I saw him lift the can of gasoline. I swear to God, I tried to get there first."

Art was still standing off a little ways, hanging back from the fire, but he trudged after them down Indigo Hill. Louisa turned to look at the shack one more time. Behind them now, the whole structure was engulfed in a tower of flame. It reached up toward the sky. Pieces of the tar-paper roof lifted off and floated down. The building seemed to be coming apart on itself, a crumbling sheet of fire and smoke.

They all stumbled back down the hill, coughing as they ran. Smoke was still curling from Flick's hair. Every rock and thorny shrub Louisa had managed to avoid on her sprint up the hill caught her on the way down. Twice she fell flat in the snow. Flick's long legs were as wobbly as a colt's, but he didn't go down once. She saw him turn his red-and-black burned face toward Paco to say something, and Paco turned his head away for a minute like he was going to be sick.

At the bottom of the hill, on Indigo Hill Road, they finally got lucky. Two older kids were heading toward them, driving along the snowy two-lane road in a four-door sedan. The headlights rose over the crest of the rise. Louisa and Paul screamed and waved their arms. The kids driving the car somehow knew enough to stop. Their car radio was blasting music. The boys staggered up to the sedan. Only Art hung back. They pulled open the back door and climbed in. Louisa leaned into the front seat and pulled the poor guy out into the cold. She thought maybe he'd been on the wrestling team at Burncoat High a couple of years before. "Get out," she commanded and she climbed inside the car.

The driver gaped at her. Art and the kid who had been in the passenger seat just stood there at the side of the road staring at them as they settled into the sedan. It was warm inside the car.

"Hospital," Flick mumbled from the back seat. His voice sounded calm, still sounded like Flick.

The driver really looked at Flick then, for the first time. "Holy shit," he said, and gunned it. They lurched off into the night. In the side-view mirror Louisa saw Art and the older boy standing at the side of the road, still staring after them. Art raised one heavy arm to wave. Louisa watched the speedometer climb to fifty, fifty-five, sixty. It occurred to her that Flick might die right there with them in the car. As they approached Shore Drive they hit a red light, with a cop car parked right next to it.

Flick leaned forward. He smelled like smoke. "Run the light," he ordered.

The driver balked. "But the police—"

"Drive!" Louisa yelled, practically into his ear. The song on the radio had changed. Someone was covering "Forever Young." The driver shook his head, but put his foot back hard on the gas.

They floated on through, running the light and sure enough, the cop pulled right after them, his red lights twirling. They sped on another half a mile or so, turning onto Route 190 where the police siren came on full blast, and flashed his lights at them, and finally they jerked over onto the shoulder of the highway, bumping over ruts.

"Shit," said the kid driving the car.

The cop got out of his patrol car. He sauntered up to their sedan. He peered inside, took one look at Flick and his whole expression changed. "Follow me!" he barked.

They flew through the cold night. Route 190 turned to 290. It felt like the car was sailing over the hills and valleys, past the Christmas lights blinking on houses, following the trail of the police car. The tires didn't seem to be touching the earth. No one talked. The radio played. The car smelled like smoke and burned flesh. They lurched and swayed with every bend in the road. Other cars' taillights sparkled. The cop kept on his siren, which almost but didn't quite drown out the wailing radio. It was still playing "Forever Young." It seemed like it would never stop playing.

Louisa thought maybe she heard Flick humming along under his breath. He must have been in shock, because he didn't seem to be in any pain yet.

Once Louisa heard him tell Paco, "I can't feel my legs."

Once Flick asked Paul Bell, "Where's Tommy? Where's your brother?" but Paul didn't answer him.

They slid along Route 290 so fast that the city seemed to zip by in a blur; with holiday lights blinking red and blue and white and green as if life was still going on as usual, and the city was festooned with its usual stars and red bows and somewhere along the line an ambulance joined in, as if they were all part of some bizarre midnight parade, and then they were suddenly stopped right in front of Memorial Hospital in Bell Hill, and hands were reaching in to pull Flick out of the car. Everything seemed to happen all at once, fast and slow at the same time, and everyone surrounding the car was dressed in blue scrubs. Louisa was shoved aside, along with Paco and Paul Bell, whose foot and hand were bleeding, and Flick was loaded onto a stretcher like a bundle of cargo. "Quit worrying," he said to Louisa.

One hospital orderly got one good look at Flick and exclaimed, "Oh my God, this kid's going to die!"

Flick opened his blackened mouth and laughed.

CHAPTER FIFTEEN

Alma Johansson floated and sank. She rose back to the surface again, gliding forward. Now and again it seemed people spoke to her and around her, in kind gentle voices, but she wasn't listening. She was dreaming her way back to her nineteenth birthday, which she had celebrated very far from home, near a small seaside city called Truro in Cornwall, England.

The parlor table was set with an oilcloth and three heavy china cups, saucers, and small round dessert plates. There was a plum cake in the middle of the table for her, for Alma. There were only three place settings—her hosts had not counted on anyone else coming—but four of them were squashed around the little table, and Mrs. Burnham rushed to set the fourth place, as if it might be bad luck, not to mention bad manners, not to have foreseen the young British soldier's presence there.

His name was Albert Dean and he was only twenty-one years old. He looked older, because his expression was nearly always serious. He was not much taller than Alma was. He and Alma were in love, though they had never spoken of this. They talked instead about the cinema shows they went to see every Saturday night. War movies and romances, mostly, and an occasional children's cartoon, just for fun. They chatted about the weather. Sometimes Albert lifted one brown, square hand and pointed out some detail about the English coastal scenery. Then they talked about the landscape. Sometimes about the kinds of seabirds.

He seemed to have the capacity to pay attention to everything around him all at once. Albert's hair was brown, his eyes the bright blue of a clear blue lake. Alma thought him the handsomest man she had ever seen—but she never let on about that, either. She could keep a secret. All four sat and ate the birthday cake in appreciative silence, with an occasional sigh or nod of approval.

Afterward, Alma walked Albert to the door. The next day he would be leaving for the Far East. His kit bag was packed, and his duffel ready, British Army issue. The situation in Korea was not terribly dangerous, and not likely to last long, but the army needed all hands on deck. He should be back in about ten months, he said. He repeated that number now, offering it like a bouquet of flowers.

"Ten months is not so long," said Alma, calculating the number in her head. She tried to convey everything possible in those six words. That she would wait. That she would not be tempted to accompany some other young man to the cinema or afterward, out to the Lymington strand or to one of the little shops or eating establishments overlooking the Isle of Wight. Not now or ever. But her heart was pounding so hard it felt as if it bounced on her tongue. She could not force any other words past.

Albert Dean appeared to study the cloud-streaked sky. He took her hand. They kept silent together a moment. He said, in his clipped, careful, timid voice, "I love you very much, Alma. And I always will. I want you to know that."

She let his words sink in, down, down, to the very core inside of her. It was the happiest moment of her young life. Every cell in her body lit up with joy. It was a moment worth celebrating, something much bigger than her birthday. In the secret cupboard of her heart she had known for some months now that Albert Dean loved her. They had ways of showing each other, of course. But hearing the words said out loud made it feel suddenly solid—not a niggling little worry, not like the uneasy way she'd been feeling almost seasick for the past few days, dizzy even when standing on dry land. As if nothing around her were solid at all.

She supposed it was the constant washing motion of the Cornish waves, all around on every side. A foreign land. The dazzle of sun, the smell of seawater and fish. It might have been her nerves, too. She was from the inland part of New England, where rivers made a long run down to the sea; she came from the thick central slice of Massachusetts. When she'd first told Albert she hailed from a place called Worcester his eyes had lit up and he'd said, "So you're English then!"

She was not English, and he was not American, but they wouldn't let that get in their way. They were so very young, and life was a great adventure.

AFTERWORD

Age shall not weary them, nor the years condemn.
At the going down of the sun and in the morning,
We will remember them.

In the winter of 1968, in Worcester, Massachusetts, a terrible tragedy took place in a neighborhood called Indian Hill, and five young people lost their lives in a fire on that hill. My fiancé, John Swenson, was one of the lucky ones who had left earlier that evening. He had been gone about twenty minutes when the entire shack went up in flames.

Indigo Hill is a work of fiction, and like all works of fiction, it is chiefly the work of imagination. I have changed a great many details to suit my story. I do this not out of disrespect for the past, but quite the opposite, to try to honor the truth by telling the best story I could make. So I have taken great liberties with facts and events, and I ask forgiveness of reality.

Many communities suffer a tragedy like the one at Indian Hill, if not in scope then in sorrow, and those whose lives it touches never forget it, even if the rest of the world may seem to march on, oblivious. I wrote this book partly to honor John and his remarkable group of friends, both the living and the dead. Nearly every family has its secrets, too. Mine is no exception. Perhaps yours is not, either. As George Bernard Shaw said, "If you cannot get rid of the family skeleton, you may as well make it dance."

ABOUT THE AUTHOR

Photo © 2015 Jonathan Cohen

Liz Rosenberg is the author of more than thirty books, including the critically acclaimed, bestselling novels *The Moonlight Palace*, *The Laws of Gravity*, and *Home Repair*. She is also a prize-winning poet and children's book author. For over twenty years, she was a book review columnist at the *Boston Globe*. She teaches creative writing and English at Binghamton University. She has also guest-taught at Bennington College, Colgate University, Sarah Lawrence College, and Queen's University in Belfast, Northern Ireland. She divides her time between Upstate New York, Florida, and Worcester, Massachusetts. She lives with her daughter, Lily, and their dog, Sophie. Her son, Eli, a comic and podcaster, lives in New York City. Visit Liz on Facebook for updates, extraordinary photos of ordinary beauty, and more information.